Aramus

Cyborgs: More Than Machines, #4

Eve Langlais

Copyright © September 2013, Eve Langlais
Cover Art by Amanda Kelsey © September
Edited by Devin Govaere
Copy Edited by Amanda Pederick
Produced in Canada

Published by Eve Langlais
1606 Main Street, PO Box 151
Stittsville, Ontario, Canada, K2S1A3
http://www.EveLanglais.com

ISBN: 978-1492781561
ISBN-10: 1492781568

Aramus is a work of fiction and the characters, events and dialogue found within the story are of the author's imagination and are not to be construed as real. Any resemblance to actual events or persons, either living or deceased, is completely coincidental.

No part of this book may be reproduced or shared in any form or by any means, electronic or mechanical, including but not limited to digital copying, file sharing, audio recording, email and printing without permission in writing from the author.

Prologue

In a time before the cyborg liberation.

The clenched fist connected with his cheek, a sturdy blow imparting decent impact and strength behind it. It wasn't enough to budge him from his post, nor did he flinch or blink.

"Holy fuck! The bastard's face is made of steel," complained the military grunt as he shook his stinging fingers.

"Must weigh a ton too," observed another soldier who stood nearby, a goading spectator since the bored crewmen began their antics. "You should have knocked him on his ass for sure with that one."

B351GI didn't twitch a single muscle or verbally respond as they discussed their attempts to harm and distract him from his current task. Cyborgs knew how to obey. *Guard the door. Do not let anyone enter.* He took his orders seriously. None would pass the perimeter while he stood watch. His directive, however, did not give instructions on how to deal with recruits who seemed to find it entertaining to see how much abuse his cyborg frame could take.

The answer? He could handle a lot, or at least more than these humans could inflict with their fleshy limbs backed by unenhanced muscles.

"Hey, Freddy, drop kick him like you did that guy last week when we raided that rebelling colony."

"Yeah, that was fucking cool," the last member of the taunting trio added. "You tossed that farmer at least six feet." He mimed a useless kick paired with a high pitched, "Hi-ya!"

Analysis of the movement deemed it unlikely that a human would have been thrown as mentioned unless done in a very low gravity area.

Freddy, a pockmarked human who did his uniform a disservice by acting in a fashion contrary to rules and regulations, did not need further encouragement. He took a step back and hopped about in place as if afflicted with a nervous system malfunction before twirling and swinging out with his foot. The steel-toed combat boot hit B351GI in the middle of his chest.

Again, had he possessed the fragile flesh and rib structure of a regular human, he would have probably suffered grievous injury. His onboard BCI—short for brain computer interface—calculated the chances of a civilian surviving such a blow at less than fifteen percent. But he was cyborg, part biological organism, part machine. He neither dented nor moved, not even to block or defend himself from attack.

His orders prevented it.

"Fuck me! The bot is like a goddamned statue!" The soldiers continued their game while B351GI stared straight ahead, ignoring them—for the moment. If they dared cross the invisible line that he guarded though...

A warning bell rang, three strident bursts, before a female computerized voice played over the onboard speakers.

"All hands to their stations. Solar flare detected. Expected time to impact, three minutes, twenty-five seconds. Initiate shut down of non-essential electronic units."

"Ah fuck, not again," grumbled Freddy. "The last one totally messed with my Samsung telecommunicator's play list."

"Don't tell me you didn't turn it off? Dude, this close to the sun, you gotta protect your electronics. You know how often it spits them flare things out."

"I know. I know. I keep forgetting."

Freddy wasn't alone in forgetting. After each solar emission, there was a complaint of something not working as it should, the electromagnetic pulse messing with the computer chips powering devices not intensely shielded by lead. Even cyborg units shut down during an event—unless there was a clear and present conflict to their standing orders, a conflict such as he faced now.

If B351GI powered off in the presence of these three soldiers, who didn't go to their duty stations as ordered, while he was incapacitated, would they use that opportunity to breach his perimeter?

It didn't take long for him to come up with an answer. His calculations on that probability came back at a sixty-three percent chance they would. Protocol was clear. Despite the incoming solar threat, he needed to remain aware, possible damage to his circuitry or not. Guarding the door and obeying was of paramount importance. Besides, B351GI did not fear the flare. They had bred trepidation and all other emotions from him when they enhanced him.

The computerized countdown continued. He didn't budge from his post or shut down any of his bodily functions. He didn't flinch even as the punching and taunting continued by the recruits as they jostled for turns trying to make him budge, their fleshly bodies unconcerned by the incoming flare.

And then it hit.

As the solar emission passed through the vessel, B351GI finally showed signs of life. He blinked. A long blink during which every atom in his being, every nerve he possessed, every circuit he owned, pulsed. Swelled. Sizzled with energy. Something within him snapped. Not audibly. Not visibly. He couldn't have said with any definitive certainty what part of him broke during that millisecond of timelessness; however, when the solar flare continued on its way, traveling thousands of miles a second, B351GI didn't feel the same.

For one thing, he *felt*. Felt the air on his skin, a hissing processed breeze of recycled air. Sensed the hum beneath his feet of the vessel as the engines rumbled, all systems a go. Heard with a clarity and, even stranger, understood the mocking tone of the three who'd kept him company during the event.

The event that changed everything and changed him. *I am broken. Or am I...*

His programming was clear in such an instance. Units who suspected defective programming or a system malfunction were to report themselves to the repair facility immediately for analysis. That was what he was supposed to do, but he didn't *feel* like it. Instead of obeying the embedded code, he made a choice. What a novelty. He *chose* to stick with his current orders. Protect the door. Let none pass.

Legs akimbo, hands loosely laced behind his back, he stared straight ahead, but he still saw the foot that rose to connect with the one fleshy part of his anatomy that, for some reason, remained intact, his testicular sac. The ankle of the soldier impacted this unprotected zone, and two things occurred.

One, the toes of his assailant crossed the invisible line as they passed between his legs—with rather painful results—into the off-limit area he guarded.

And two…

"That fucking hurt," said B351GI in a gravelly voice he'd not used since they embedded the wireless receiver and transmitter in his body. His observation stood out, stark and distinctive, even amidst the jocularity of those toying with him. Silence settled. Three sets of eyes swung his way, the whites wide.

"Did the cyborg just speak?" The private stood slack-jawed, staring at him.

"Nah. Can't be. They can't do nothing, not even take a piss, unless they have orders to," said Freddy with brash assurance.

"I'm telling you it spoke," insisted his companion.

"And I'm telling it didn't."

"Prove it. Kick it in the balls again. I dare you!"

And there was error number three. B351GI didn't want to experience anew the discomfort that still radiated from his tender sac, not to mention Freddy, with malicious intent, intended to cross the line, *his* line, again.

B351GI caught the foot before it hit and held it in an iron-clad grip.

"Let me go, motherfucker," Freddy yelled, as he hopped in an attempt to retain his precarious balance.

Poor Freddy. He didn't have the clearance to give him orders. "I don't think so." It didn't take much to twist and break the offending limb. Just like it didn't take much expended energy or effort to silence the screaming. A twist of the neck, a sharp crack, and Freddy stared with sightless orbs. Such an inefficient unit who'd ended up paying the penalty for disobeying orders.

Of course, his companions didn't see it that way.

"You cyborg bastard. You killed Freddy."

Yes. Yes, he had. He mulled his choices, again a new thing for him, about whether to reply or not. He chose to give an explanation. "He crossed the line."

His answer did not placate them. Profanities frothed at their lips as they backed away with wild eyes and spitted invectives. The remaining pair drew their weapons, laser pistols not meant to be used on board ships in transit, only planet-side where they wouldn't cause an accidental hull breach. Yet again another example of the recruits' poor training and inability to obey the most basic of rules.

B351GI pointed this out. "The use of plasma firearms is prohibited under section eighty-three, sub section six A of the onboard protocol manual. Please sheathe your weapons." He couched it politely, as per his programming.

The soldiers continued to aim the weapons, threatening to shoot. His BCI analyzed the situation. Threat to his well-being? Vaguely important. His prime directive stated human life ranked above that of a cyborg. But what about his orders? If B351GI ended up incapacitated, his post would be left unguarded. This ranked as very important. *I cannot let them kill me.* Never mind the fact he felt a need to survive or to protect himself, protocol would save him.

Odd how a sensation of enjoyment imbued him at the thought. Or he assumed what he felt was joy, given half of his mouth curled in what his databanks defined as a smirk of amusement.

"So be it." He couldn't say with any definitive authority that he enjoyed disarming the humans and rendering them incapable of breaching his post. They didn't pose enough of a challenge for that. However, an inner part of him chuckled, darkly, perhaps even maliciously, when hours later the officer who'd given him the order to stand guard came striding up the hall. Lieutenant Wilson blanched as his gaze alit upon the bodies.

"What the hell happened here?"

B351GI didn't blink or move.

"I asked you a direct question, cyborg. What happened here?" It seemed his lieutenant forgot for a moment whom he spoke to. It didn't take him long to remember. He smacked a wall. "Fucking mute robot units. Safety feature my ass. And of course the onboard communication device is down."

B351GI decided to aid his obviously beleaguered commanding officer. "They breached the line, sir. I took care of it."

Apparently, replying, and his actions in regards to the breach, weren't correct. Declared defective, despite what B351GI thought, the lieutenant marched him to the utility bay where the mechanic declared him unfit for duty. They judged him dangerous to humans and slated him for termination. B351GI disagreed with their assessment. Actually, he disagreed with a lot of things the humans did. So, he stopped listening to them and stopped obeying their orders. He no longer cared what the humans thought or wanted. He ignored them, even when they begged for their lives as he killed them.

Along with some of his other enlightened brothers, B351GI freed himself and made a vow as he stood amidst the blood and carnage, basking in the victory of his liberation.

No human shall ever control me again. And those who try, will die.

Chapter One

Years later, on the cyborg homeworld…

"What do you mean Seth is missing?" Aramus barked.

Holding up a hand did nothing to stem the cacophony of questions that came flying from all directions by those present at the hastily gathered meeting. Joe waited for silence before answering. "I'd think my words were very clear. Seth is missing, as in he is no longer on this planet."

"Is he dead?"

Negative according to Joe's shaken head.

"But how and when? We just arrived," Aphelion noted, an unneeded observation since all present were well aware of that obvious fact.

Joe shrugged in a much-too-humanlike manner. "I'm unsure of the exact time, but it appears to be not long after the arrival of the *SSBiteMe,* carrying your crew, Aramus, and our newest addition, Bonnie."

Brows beetling together, Aramus glared at the troublesome female who'd vexed him during the voyage. "I knew she was a traitor! Let's kill her now."

His logical solution did not go unchallenged. Einstein jumped from his seat and stood in front of Bonnie. "Like hell! Bonnie couldn't have played a part in Seth's disappearance because she's been with me the entire time."

"Maybe she was communicating with whoever did this."

"Without a wireless transmitter?" Einstein scoffed.

"There is more than one way to send messages. I don't know how she did it, but I'm sure she's somehow to blame." She was certainly to blame for the glue in Aramus's boots, which had taken hours of soaking in a chemical solution to remove, and for the bubbles he'd belched when she handed him a bottle of water on the ship filled with liquid soap. She and the others giggled at her so-called pranks. Aramus thought they hid a devious, conniving mind, one determined to send his circuits into a closed loop, the cyborg version of insanity.

Bonnie snorted. "Sorry, grumpy one, but you're really grasping at straws. Instead of jumping to conclusions and letting your paranoia control you, which, by the way, they sell aluminum hats for, why not let the big boys, you know, the ones who think with actual brains instead of metal lumps, talk?"

"One, everyone knows you need a lead hat to block mind control." He'd looked it up the first time she used that particular insult on him. "And two—"

"There is no two because you know I had nothing to do with it because if I had, Joe here would have already slapped me in chains."

Damn, he hated it when she made sense. Joe would never let her roam around free if he suspected her, a fact Joe reinforced with a wireless message of, *She's not responsible. So sit down, shut up, and listen.*

"You are a pain in my iron-clad ass," Aramus grumbled as he dropped back into his seat. Despite his quick-tempered outburst, logic dictated Bonnie, the newest cyborg female to join their society, didn't have anything to do with Seth's disappearance. He still was of the mind they should kill her, but less because he thought she was a traitor and more because he hated that she'd stolen Einstein to the dark side, the side of—ugh—love. It was almost like a rampant disease taking good cyborg soldiers and turning them into caring beings. It made them human instead of practical. It made Aramus want to throw up the digestive acid in his stomach.

What was it about this whole love thing that took perfectly good soldiers and turned them into human shadows of themselves? Aramus thought it should more aptly be defined as lust with a dose of madness, but no one listened to him. Hell, they all kept threatening to find him a woman of his own who'd change his mind. He'd rather donate his parts for recycling first.

Was it any wonder he wanted to save his friend from the clutches of the emasculating emotion? He knew many would recommend he be sent for a reboot for thinking this way, but he couldn't help it. He hated all things human, especially emotions. With Seth's disappearance, he'd seen an opportunity to free his friend Einstein from Bonnie's clutches, a plan that failed. But, at least he'd tried, even if it was too late. She'd already completely corrupted him.

Joe took control of the meeting with a fist slammed down on the boardroom table. Good thing they'd built it sturdy because it wasn't a gentle thud, and the loud noise cut through the chaos. An instant hush settled. "Everyone calm the hell down. As I was saying before I was interrupted," Joe glared at Aramus, who subtly scratched his chin with his middle finger, "Seth is missing. And, no, Bonnie isn't to blame. According to the short message I received, from Seth himself I might add, Seth left willingly. He just wouldn't say with who."

"You mean he wasn't alone?" Aramus picked apart Joe's words.

"No, he wasn't."

"So who of our ranks is also unaccounted for?"

"No one."

Again a barrage of questions fired at their leader from all directions. Joe held up his hand and got the quiet he wanted. "I know you all have questions. So do I. But at this point, I don't have answers. All I know is Seth has departed the planet and he was not alone."

"He left with a stranger?"

"Again, I don't know. He would not elaborate. All I can confirm is whomever he vanished with is not anyone currently registered with the cyborg census bureau."

Aphelion interrupted. "I have a different question no one seems to have asked. How? How did he leave? How did this mysterious person contact him? How did any of this happen without us knowing about it?"

Joe's fists clenched on the tabletop under the barrage of questions. "I'm afraid we've no answers yet to any of those questions."

"You mean, you don't know? How is this possible?" Einstein's interest was evident in the way his mechanical eyes glowed, and he craned forward, his curious nature piqued.

"Are we even sure he's left the surface?"

"Yes."

"If he's not on the planet, then he obviously used some form of transportation."

"A valid assumption except our tracking devices caught no indication whatsoever of any incoming craft or communications. And trust me when I say I've had them going over our readings of the last few days in case we missed something. Despite the illogicalness of it, Seth is most definitely gone. Left the planet, somehow and without us detecting a thing."

Which made no plausible sense. They had the most advanced detection system humanity had to offer. Better actually, given they'd made modifications and improvements courtesy of their cyborg intelligence and innovation. Nothing could get past them, or at least, nothing should have.

The implication chilled even a tough-as-a-steel-girder bastard like Aramus who didn't feel much. If someone could come amongst them, close enough to snag one of their most capable soldiers, then what else were they capable of? It almost didn't bear thinking of. A rational explanation had to exist. Somehow, somewhere, someone had overlooked a crucial fact.

"Are you trying to claim he pulled a Houdini? That he magically teleported himself elsewhere?" Aramus couldn't help the caustic reply as his BCI searched for a way to reconcile the facts with the situation—and failed.

"Logic states it's impossible he left without a trace, yet we cannot refute the evidence. But I wouldn't go so far as to call it magic."

"Could his disappearance be linked to more of that peculiar technology the military seems to have gotten its hands on, perhaps?" Einstein mused aloud.

"You think they've come up with some kind of teleportation device?"

"Or a really sophisticated cloaking one. One only has to recall that tracking device we found, the one we could not detect or feel but only see, to realize the possibility exists."

"Speaking of which, have you made any headway on that?" Joe directed his question to their resident cybernetic geek.

Einstein shook his head. "None. I've dismantled the bug and put it under every microscope we have and through every test I can think of. Not only is the technology unknown, so are the metals and polymers it's comprised of. I haven't yet had a chance to run tests on the items and readings from our most recent encounter with the technology, but if I were to make a completely wild guess—"

"Since when do we guess?" Aramus retorted.

Einstein continued as if he hadn't heard. "Then I'd have to say, inconceivable as it seems, that it is alien in origin."

"Alien as in new and never seen before?" Aphelion queried.

Einstein shook his head. "No, I mean alien as in non-human in origin. I don't know how, but I think our military has stumbled upon advanced extraterrestrial life, or at least their technology."

"No fucking way," Aramus exclaimed.

"Why not?" Kyle asked. Known as the questioner, he'd often declared himself a believer in life on other planets, even if they'd yet to encounter anything smarter or larger than a horse.

Take their current home. While it boasted life, of the four- to eight-legged, furry to scaly variety, none of it showed more than a modicum of intelligence. Definitely nothing along the lines of the intelligence evolved in humans.

"I'll tell you why not, because there is no way the military could keep a lid on something this big. Don't forget, we know how things work on bases, even secret ones. Soldiers talk. They talk to their wives. Their lovers. Rumors, especially about something this momentous, would have seeped out."

"And yet they kept the secret of how they created us and what they did to us from the majority of humans until our public acts of retaliation could be hidden no longer."

Heads nodded all around.

"Proving my point," Aramus said.

"Not really. We went public, and once we did, they manipulated the media into seeing us as monsters, attributing any event where humans died as part of a cyborg plot to overthrow humanity."

"What if it's not the military who got their hands on this alien technology?" Chloe, silent up until now, spoke softly, yet everyone heard. "What if it's the *others*, the ones funding the cyborg project. The company did a pretty decent job of hiding the fact they'd made female units. If they got their hands on alien technology, want to bet they'd do their utmost to keep it secret, even from the military?"

"It's possible."

Even Aramus couldn't deny she might have a point. The unknown and secret corporation, who banked the effort to create, then eradicate, cyborgs, definitely had the money to cover up and the facilities to hide something like ET's. The fact that it had ended up in military hands and on a military craft could just be the result of them selling their adaptations to any who could afford it.

Bonnie clapped her hands. "This is so awesome. Maybe we'll finally get to meet some green Martians!"

"We have no way of knowing what they look like or the color of their exterior casing." Einstein, as usual, stuck to the facts, and Bonnie stuck out her tongue. A tender smile, which made Aramus slightly nauseous, tilted Einstein's lips. "But even without knowing their physical makeup, I do believe given what we've encountered and learned so far that the technology we are dealing with is most definitely not from Earth."

This time the cacophony of voices could not be restrained as the cyborgs present all voiced their opinions, some aloud, some amongst each other via their wireless communicators.

Via mind-to-mind contact was how Aramus queried Joe. *Do you believe what Einstein says?*

Actually, I do. It would make sense of a lot of what we've encountered lately and some of the messages we've intercepted.

How though? And how could we not have heard about this before? We've been roaming the galaxy for years, and we've never encountered anything that has remotely hinted that anyone else with space-faring ability inhabits the areas we've explored.

Perhaps nothing does, but we've only visited a fraction of planets and solar systems. Who can really say what exists out there? Perhaps through some fluke or wormhole, an alien vessel somehow ended up in human hands. Depending on the technology they were dealing with, it might not have been too hard to adopt or adapt their findings.

I don't like it.

Neither do I, but at least it gives us something to work with.

How do you figure? We have only bits and pieces of the alien junk, and nobody to dissect for intel. Or kill. Right about now, given his level of frustration, Aramus would have dearly loved something to use as target practice, say something in a military uniform.

That's where you're wrong. We do have a lead of sorts. I didn't want to relay this to the general populace, but Seth's message contained a little bit more than I conveyed. He also left coordinates.

To what?

That he didn't specify, other than to indicate we would find some answers if we went there. He also stated that we should do so promptly, and expect resistance.

Aramus didn't hesitate. *I'll do it.*

How did I know you'd say that?

Because Aramus never turned down an opportunity to fight, or kill, humans. He lived to hear them scream, lived to make them pay, and enjoyed the fear in their eyes as they faced their mortality as they paid for their crimes against him and his brothers.

When do I leave?

Slow down.

I thought you said the message demanded promptness.

It does, but I also don't want to send you off half-cocked and poorly staffed. Or have you so soon forgotten the fiasco of your last mission?

Ah yes, the betrayal of their kind by one of the crew. He'd died for his actions, but his defection had been a sobering reminder that not all cyborgs lived for their revolution and that they weren't immune to blackmail.

So, I'll handpick the crew. I trust Aphelion and Einstein.

You can't have Einstein. I need him here in his lab deciphering the mystery of these artifacts.

And so he and Joe bartered back and forth before settling on a small crew of eight plus Aramus. Eight cyborgs who possessed no ties either here on the cyborg homeworld or back on earth. Eight soldiers who'd proven themselves in battle against the humans. Eight of the best with Aramus to lead them.

There was no fanfare to their departure. No announcement or warning. They simply lifted off, on a mission into the unknown, facing danger yet to be determined, on a quest for who knew what.

Some days it was great being a murderous cyborg given free license to cause mayhem and havoc. Aramus almost bared his metallic choppers in an elated grin. *This is a mission I have a feeling I'm going to enjoy.*

Chapter Two

"What are you waiting for? Cut him open already." The voice barked right in her ear, and Riley flinched, the small jerk causing the laser she wielded to zigzag across the flesh she dissected.

Oops. She braced for the slap, which surprisingly didn't follow. Instead, she received a verbal version.

"You stupid bitch. Can't you do anything right?"

Inwardly, she seethed—*Pompous prick!*—outwardly, she cringed. "I-I'm sorry. You startled me. Don't worry, I didn't damage anything of import." As if the dead thing on her table cared.

Where the company and the military kept finding these mutant bodies and why they kept shipping them to her dead, were questions she'd learned not to ask. The first beating had taught her that lesson. The subsequent ones made sure she understood she lived and breathed only so long as they found her useful. Fighting back wasn't an option, not without weapons or a small army, and she wasn't stupid enough to cause trouble. She'd noted what happened to those who fought or mouthed off. They left, usually kicking and screaming, in the grips of mercenaries and soldiers who didn't care—and they never came back.

As she peeled back the skin and muscles from the chest area of her specimen, she began her monotonous discourse on her findings, knowing everything was being recorded both audibly and visually for scientists back home. It seemed whatever had transformed these poor souls into monsters, was something to be feared or hidden. God forbid they accidentally introduced a mutant virus to earth. Better to do their research off-planet with a small team—an expendable team, which included her, willing or not. She didn't get the impression though, what they dealt with was that contagious, given no one wore hazmat suits and the only decontamination she underwent was when they moved her from the transport ship to the company facility. She still shivered remembering the coldness of the spray. It seemed expendables, like herself, didn't rate warm water. *Not to mention they took away my liberty and rights.* But to whom could she complain?

"As with the other subjects, the specimen maintains most of the physical markers of *homo sapiens* with slight variations. I count fourteen pairs of ribs, the bone thicker than that of a human, and longer. The ends are fused together on seven of the sets forming an actual cage. The makeup of the skeletal structure is consistent with *homo sapiens*, with this specimen showing only two arms and legs, their structure implying a bipedal nature. They are however, comprised of an unknown material, a dark gray in color with a less porous texture than that of human bone. Further testing is required to elaborate on the actual substance. It should be noted that whatever the bone is comprised of, it is very durable, resisting impact and even deflecting attempts to cut by the power tools available to me." The toughness of the skeletal structure often made her think of Wolverine with his adamantine bones. *Except these guys aren't as hot.*

As she itemized her findings, many of the aspects identical to other corpses she'd dissected before, she let her mind wander. After all, the novelty of discovering what hid beneath the epidermis of what, at first glance, appeared alien skin had worn off after the first few bodies.

To think she'd been so excited when they'd given her the first one, back when she believed she was a valued team member.

"A mutant human? What do you mean? Are we talking an X-Men-type being or something else?" She'd regarded her superior at the military run medical research center she worked for with disbelief, certain her coworkers played a joke.

"Definitely something else. This is, of course, classified info. What I'm about to reveal to you goes no farther than this office. Understood?"

She nodded. She remembered well the clause in her contract that dealt with confidentiality. "I understand."

"Excellent. We've gotten our hands on a corpse that is human in origin, but, at the same time, not. We want you to examine the remains."

Less examine than study it, looking for weaknesses and strengths. It didn't take long for her to discover that the bodies on her autopsy table hadn't died via natural means or by accident. The bullet holes through their eye sockets—because the skulls were too tough—made that glaringly evident.

Back then, months and months ago, when she still believed she worked for the greater good, she sought to question, to demand answers. It was then she discovered that in some places the laws meant nothing. She meant nothing, and some people hid beneath a polite veneer to camouflage their evil nature. It still shocked her the way the most seemingly benign people could mete out violence without fear of repercussion. People so rotten to the core that they thought nothing of threatening her with horrible things, of carrying out torture in order to ensure her obedience.

Forget going for help or reporting the perpetrators to the authorities. As soon as she balked at their demands and actions, they'd imprisoned her. No trial. No phone calls. Nothing. They kept her from her family and cut off any and all contact with the outside world. Then they'd moved her off-planet.

A respected forensic anthropologist back on earth, and they'd just erased all her rights, kidnapping and bringing her to her current location, buried inside a mountain on a planet thought inhabitable. Forget the bright future and life she'd once led. Now, she was little more than a prisoner with no hope of escape or rescue. No one knew where she was in the galaxy, and even if she could get the word out, who would save her? Her family couldn't exactly mount a rescue mission to the outer reaches of the galaxy. Nor did she dare put them in danger by identifying her captors. The military and the company—a secret organization that had no name—wielded the power to let her loved ones live or die, just like they controlled her life.

But not my mind! While outwardly she appeared cooperative, inside, she plotted their demise. Of course, in her fantasy, she was a kick-ass heroine wielding a huge, freaking gun, screaming "Freedom" as she blew the bastards away. In reality, she'd probably play the part of a peeing-her-pants weakling hiding under the nearest table.

God, I hate my life.

At least, unlike some of the other female prisoners, she didn't have to deal with rape. Apparently, she was too precious for that. They needed her mind intact to do her work and not have her a blubbering, suicidal mess. How smacking her around and beating her was any better she'd yet to figure out, but apparently, so long as she could stand and wield a scalpel, punishment was acceptable—whether it was deserved or not.

If only she weren't so cowardly, she would have taken her own life, turned the knife on herself, spite them with their own tools. But, she wanted to live, even if her life wasn't worth much. In spite of all she'd suffered, they couldn't extinguish the spark within her that refused to go out, a spark of hope, even if she'd given up on praying. She'd seen too much evil at this point to believe in God anymore. What god allowed men to perpetuate such vileness? None that she knew of and none she wished to know. And most definitely none she would ever worship.

The sudden blaring of horns startled them all. It was the first time since her arrival that she'd heard them, and she couldn't help asking, "What are those for?"

For once, her query didn't meet with a cuff to the side of her head.

"We're under attack." How incredulous her jailor sounded, and with reason.

From what she'd gleaned, since her arrival several months back, their facility was hidden on a planet considered uninhabitable by humans. Camouflaged within a rocky mountain, with only the barest of traffic allowed in or out under the guise of taking surface readings, no one should have known they existed. The company and the military had made sure of that.

And yet someone had come snooping.

Whoever it is, I hope they kill this bastard. The bastard in question, Arthur Dennison, who took perverse delight in tormenting her, shoved her out of his way instead of going around. The jolt rammed her into the unforgiving surface of the autopsy table and bruised her hip. She dared a glare at his retreating back. *Make that, I hope he dies painfully.* A glorified pencil pusher, he held no medical degree or military rank, but for some reason, he was her supervisor, and a sadistic prick. He'd made it his personal mission to make her life a living hell.

Dragged back to her cell by excited mercenaries who chattered in a language not English, she made no attempt to fight or get away. If they were under attack, then she'd rather hide. In a battle she would only get underfoot. She was better off waiting it out and hoping that whoever invaded came to save and not just destroy. *Because anything has to be better than this hell.*

Chapter Three

If I believed in Hell, it would probably look like this planet. Or so Aramus thought as he got his first glimpse of the blistering surface of his destination.

He double-checked the coordinates. They were correct. *Did Seth send us on a wild chase?* It wouldn't be the first time the damnable cyborg had played a prank.

This fucking overgrown asteroid isn't hiding a secret. Unless it was one of how to survive on a planet comprised mostly of volcanic rock, lava, and smoke. Nothing organic could exist on its surface. Even cyborgs, versatile bastards that they were, would find the excessive heat more than their circuits could handle. But, within the stone…that proved a different story.

"Sir, I'm detecting faint radio waves emitting from the large mountain the coordinates have led us to."

"Can we tell who they belong to, Kentry?" Aramus asked his communications officer. Who as in military, civilian or pirate. None of them were cyborg friends, but at least in the case of civilian, they could usually bluff their way to getting what they needed. A reputation as killers came in handy at times.

"I believe it's a mixture of all three, sir."

"Explain.

"I'm picking up traces of Russian, Spanish, English, and the use of military jargon. I think. The magnetic properties of the stone are making it difficult for me to get a more accurate recording."

"Bring up the planet's statistics again."

On screen, there appeared a recap of what they knew, facts that his BCI already had stored. However, Aramus sometimes found it easier to spot items of interest when given a visual representation.

Discovered less than ten years ago, the planet, dubbed Pahoehoe, rotated on a figure eight axis around two stars, close enough to make the surface a melting, hot mess. Weak in metals, with no sign of life or water, the planet had been deemed unfit for colonization and useless for mining. In other words, it was junk.

He returned to a specific entry, actually, a specific name. "General Boulder signed off on this planet? He was the one to designate it non-inhabitable?" Now that was interesting. Knee deep in the cyborg program, General Boulder was a top player, which in turn, meant anything revolving around this particular general raised a red flag.

"Yes, sir."

"So here we've got a useless planet, and yet, according to the space logs we stole a while back from that military freighter, there have been regular visits to it, supposedly to get readings. Readings of what? How fucking hot it is?"

"No idea, sir. But it does seem suspicious. Should we sweep in for a closer look?"

"No. We're already close enough as it is. Here's to hoping they don't have any of that fancy new technology, or any hope of surprising them is already lost. Park us out of sight, Aphelion."

"Aye aye, captain."

Smartass. Once the most serious of cyborgs, ever since the stint of time spent in Bonnie's presence, Aphelion sported a more relaxed method of speech and mannerisms. Curse the humans and their habits that seemed to spread like a virus, corrupting perfectly decent, mission-oriented units. Thank fuck Aramus held better control over his actions. He wouldn't succumb to useless emotions. He'd give himself a lobotomy first.

Circling to the far side of the questionable mountain and its mysterious emissions, Aramus and his crew held a mini meeting to decide their next move.

"I say we go in guns blazing." Xylo, like Aramus, preferred the direct approach.

"We don't know what we're facing. We could end up walking into a trap." Aphelion, as usual, proved the annoying voice of reason.

"Just in case we're dealing with aliens, we should try making contact first," interjected Kentry, who, like Kyle, believed in the whole alien scenario.

"I doubt we're dealing with ETs," Aramus stated. "Or have you forgotten the reports of survey vessels going in and out of this area, not to mention the speech patterns we've picked up?"

"Speaking of getting in, where would we penetrate?" Kyle raised the most important question. Given they didn't know what to expect, they couldn't just blast a hole in the mountain to pay its occupants a visit. Not if they intended to rescue or question anything inside.

"I'm not detecting a landing zone in the area large enough for a spacecraft. While they could be dropping supplies in, it seems unlikely given the high winds could carry their cargo right into a crevice where recovery would prove impossible. There's got to be a hidden entrance of some kind. Some kind of bay doors to let the ships in," Kentry replied as he pored over an aerial map.

Aramus snorted. "Hidden or not, it does us no good. It's not like we can just walk up to their front door, knock, and ask for entry. Given the lengths they've gone to to hide it, I'm sure they have a shoot-first policy in place." He knew he would. "That said, though, if this installation is built along more or less traditional lines, then they'll have at least two access points. A large one for vessels or cargo and a smaller entrance, on the opposite side or not so close, that can be used in an emergency for escape." Because, as humans learned early on when building within mountains and planets, if shit hit the fan, having only one exit during a calamity ensured an almost hundred-percent fatality rate for humans. Especially if cyborgs controlled that exit and decided to not let anyone pass. Aramus almost smiled in fond recollection at the invasion of the military base on the fifth moon circling Saturn. What a fun time he'd had.

"Scanning the mountain for a concentrated area of metal indicating a portal," Kyle announced, his eyes staring off for a moment as he set his inner BCI to the task.

"Once we do find our way in, what are we looking for?" Xylo asked. "You haven't told us much."

"Because we don't know much. You are all aware Seth disappeared?" Heads nodded all around. "Well, before he did, he gave Joe a message telling us to come here. That we'd find some of the answers we seek at this location."

"Answers to what?"

Aramus shrugged. "I can't tell you because I don't know. All I know is apparently we should expect some kind of resistance, but at the same time, we need to not eradicate everyone in our path, as we might need to question them." A waste of oxygen if you asked Aramus. The only good human was a dead one. Then they couldn't spin lies to justify their actions.

"So we should set our weapons to stun and incapacitate?"

He nodded. "But, if your life is in danger, do not hesitate to use deadly force. A cyborg life is worth more than any human's."

"I found the entrances!" Kyle interrupted. "Take a look."

Making use of the holographic technology embedded in the table of the meeting room, Kyle pulled up a three-dimensional image of the mountain. It rotated slowly on its axis, a perfect composite drawing that showed every nook, cranny, and abnormality on its surface. Shading of a different color showed density of the rock while minerals and metals appeared as different hues. It wasn't hard to spot the service bay doors. Their big purple outline stood out in stark contrast to the rest of the diagram, but it was the two smaller portals to the east and south of the mountain that truly grabbed their attention.

"As you can see," Kyle stated while pointing unnecessarily, "there are two doors, here and here. The east one seems to be where they dump their garbage. Scans of the area show tread marks and piles of ash from the burning of trash."

"What about the south entrance?"

"Seems like it's currently unused, probably because a lava channel, a recent one according to previous surveys of the area I found stored, decided to run a path too close to the entrance." While environmental suits could handle high temperatures, lava was too much for them. Lava was too much for anything, even cyborgs, who could handle extreme conditions.

"South entrance it is. We'll need some kind of diversion to keep their attention away from that area, as we can't land close by and will need to travel by either foot or small craft to our target zone."

"I think I can easily arrange a diversion." Aphelion actually smiled and even cracked his knuckles in a human-like gesture that made Aramus frown. "I'll take the ship in for a closer peek and try to hail them. That should get their alarms screaming and grab their attention."

"While the humans are keeping an eye on the front, we'll sneak in the back."

A sound plan. A perfect plan. One that went off as intended, without a hitch. How boring.

Let off behind a volcano about three miles from their target, and dressed in suits made to withstand extreme heat, including some annoying helmets, Aramus and his infiltration team, comprised of himself and five of the crew, waited for the signal.

We've been noticed, Aphelion messaged him. *They have not responded, but their communication channels have all gone silent. I'm going to keep hailing and demand entry.*

Excellent. *Move!* Aramus sent the message via their neural interface, their proximity not affected by the strong and disruptive magnetic properties of the planet. Given the low gravity, they'd opted to not use an all-terrain vehicle and instead, relied on their space training and innate acrobatic skills to get them across the hostile surface quickly. Running and leaping, they bounded from rock to crag, the low gravity giving them momentum and height. They bounced over streaming rivulets of molten rock to land on porous shores, only to jump again, making their way rapidly overland.

A more poetic cyborg might have admired the harsh landscape, its red hues where heat predominated contrasting with the dark where the heat had waned, leaving behind twisted formations, pockmarked with air bubbles. Despite himself and his dislike of all things that reminded him of humans, Aramus couldn't help but contrast the scenery once again with that of the biblical Hell most religions believed in. *The only thing missing is some evil military grunts chained to the rocks tortured by devils.*

He'd gladly play the part of demon if he could find a human or two to punish.

Hoping Aphelion had managed to keep the humans' attention, Aramus and the others reached the southern entrance. Without hesitation, Kentry went to work on the door, yanking off the control panel and slicing through wires. First, he disarmed any alarms opening the portal would set off, and then he began fiddling with the circuits, needing to create a manual override that allowed him to slide the door open. In they piled, crowding the pressure chamber, but they wanted to waste as little time as possible when they breached the inner door to the installation itself. Kentry slapped the inner button, and the exit to the surface slid shut. Air hissed as the room pressure stabilized.

"On my count," Aramus muttered, keeping an eye on the clock. "Three, two, one." Pressure equalized, the door swung open, and they dove out into the larger service chamber, rolling and bounding to their feet, weapons pointed at…nothing. It seemed their arrival went unnoticed. While a distant alarm clanged, no attacking force waited to greet them.

What a shame. Nothing like starting a mission off with some head-bashing and shooting to get the blood pumping.

The portal to the outdoor chamber clanged as it slid shut. "Spread out. Mute all communications unless it's an emergency. Remember what I said about casualties. If you can take those you come across prisoner, great, if not…" He shrugged. "Don't let them scream and warn the others."

"And most of all, have fun!" Xylo couldn't help adding, his visor hiding the grin they could all hear in his voice.

Their dark chuckles echoed in the dusty space but cut off as soon as they hit the exits, one to the left and one to the right. Where they'd end up and what they'd find was anyone's guess.

Aramus jogged ahead, leader of his group, gun loosely held in one hand, a knife in the other. He'd found for close-quarter combat a blade did a better job than firearms. It didn't give the same satisfaction as using his bare fists, but when it came to efficiency, he liked the silence and projectile ability of a good knife. Not all of his kind shared his preference. Some units had grown soft since their liberation and eschewed weapons with sharp edges, claiming they were too messy. Aramus didn't know what their problem was. A little bit of cold water always rinsed the blood out.

The corridor they traversed was rough in the extreme with the height varying from a lofty ten feet plus to, at times, a hunched-over five. The surface was porous rock with lights embedded at intervals with the floor underfoot sporting some kind of rubbery layer that made the lumps and bumps less noticeable. By his observation, the tunnel was natural not manmade, old lava routes long since cooled that had left behind a maze of corridors and chambers, one of which they spilled into, surprising the staff clearing the dishes from the latest meal. Gun already set on stun, Aramus simply aimed and fired, dropping the chubby human before he could open his mouth to yell. Kentry immobilized the younger one, who, hands full with a basin of dishes, hit the floor with a clatter.

Aramus turned to glare at his compatriot.

Kentry lifted his hands in an 'oops' gesture meant to placate. Aramus growled. Using the zip ties they'd brought along, he bound the hands and ankles of their first two victims—one hundred percent human, not alien much to Kentry's disappointment—while Xylo and Kentry checked the kitchen area for more staff. They emerged with two bodies slung over their shoulders and sported looks of disgust.

"What's wrong?" Aramus whispered. "Did they give you trouble or sound an alarm?"

"These fucking shits over here had these two women chained to the fucking counter like animals," Xylo snarled. "And, no, they didn't scream. They can't. The bastards rendered them mute."

Sure enough, when Kentry and Xylo gently placed their burdens down, the faces of the women, even in repose, wore lines of fear and anxiety. And no wonder. Aramus could see the scars on their throats, two tiny slits that incapacitated their voice boxes. He also noted the bruising on their legs, arms, and faces. Victims of the bastards in charge. To think humans called cyborgs brutes.

"I stunned them because I wasn't sure what to do," Kentry explained almost apologetically. "I don't think they would have sounded an alarm, but then again, we are big, bad cyborgs."

Big and bad indeed. Even though they kept their killing to the military, the company, and those attacking them while leaving civilians, women, and children alone, humans preferred to believe the false media reports that portrayed them as out-of-control killers. Aramus especially enjoyed the documentary that claimed they kidnapped healthy humans to use for spare parts. As if they'd taint their enhanced bodies with substandard fleshy issue.

"Do we tie them up like the others?" Kentry asked.

It seemed cruel even to him to subject these undernourished females to the same treatment as their abusers, yet he knew from experience that even victims could cause trouble if not properly subdued. "Until we have the place secured, no one, not even prisoners, can be allowed free rein."

Appearing unhappy about it, but ever an obedient soldier, Kentry knelt and did as told before they went on their way.

Their next encounter occurred in a dorm, a large room with about a dozen bunks, only a handful of which were occupied. Taking out the groggy mercs—who were too hung over to respond to the alarm asking all hands to report for duty—proved easy. Knocking out the female they discovered there, who fell to her knees before them with tears streaming down dirty cheeks, was much harder. Whether she was human or not, Aramus couldn't help but feel pity for her. He didn't like it one bit.

The next group they came across, actual guards armed with weapons, didn't get the same mercy as those they'd already found. Aramus justified their deaths with the fact they aimed their weapons. That it gave him satisfaction to terminate some of those involved in the torture of the females didn't factor into the equation at all.

"Shall we see what these two were guarding?" he asked before blowing the lock off the door.

What he found almost put him on his knees and exploded his already simmering temper.

Chapter Four

"Holy fuck, it's Avion." Kentry whispered his observation.

"I thought he died in that asteroid attack months ago." Even the usually loud Xylo kept his voice hushed.

Aramus tuned his comrades out as he stared at the cyborg chained to the rock wall, a cyborg he knew well. A cyborg they'd all thought dead. A friend who'd instead been tortured and experimented on to the point he appeared as only a shadow of himself. Gaunt didn't come close to describing this formerly virile unit. Avion's muscles appeared atrophied, his skin brittle, his hair tangled and dirty. Aramus couldn't help but feel pity at his emaciated appearance.

What happened to him?

Cyborgs could handle a lot of punishment. Their ability to turn their pain receptors on or off helped with that. They could also derive nourishment from just about any situation, their skin absorbing nutrients and metals from their surroundings, meaning they should never starve. But not so in Avion's case. What had they done to this once strong cyborg?

Tucking his gun in his waistband, Aramus approached Avion, who flinched when he laid his hands on him. "Brother. We've come to liberate you."

Raising his head slowly, hanks of stringy unwashed and uncombed hair covering parts of his face, Avion faced him, and Aramus held in a shudder because even he, who'd seen so much, was shocked. His poor friend.

Eyeless sockets faced him, while cuts, open and unhealed, crisscrossed a face mottled with bruises.

"Aramus?" Avion croaked.

"Yes, it's me. I'm going to get you out of here. Hold on while I take care of your tethers."

"Electric," Avion gasped.

The warning came too late. Aramus had already gripped a wrist restraint, and as soon as he made contact with the metal, the energy coursing through it jumped into his body, volts and volts of it. Hands tugged him free of the circuit.

Having conditioned himself to withstand current—a conditioning that had taken him months as he shocked himself over and over—he didn't fall. But neither was Aramus completely unaffected. He shook his head and wavered on his feet as his nanobots went to work repairing the damage to his neural system as quickly as they could.

"Holy fuck. No wonder he can't break free. They've got enough juice running through him to kill him."

"Not kill. Experiment," Avion whispered. "Always testing."

"Testing for what?" But his friend didn't answer. Avion's chin hit his chest as he lost consciousness or rebooted. Either way, he didn't suffer at the moment. "Kentry, find the switch and turn the electricity off. I think we've just found what we were looking for."

"Don't be so sure," Xylo announced from the hall. He poked his head in. "I saw a screen in the hall and pulled up a map of the installation. According to the schematic and the work roster, there's about fifteen other guarded cells."

"With cyborgs inside?"

"I don't know. I couldn't get past their firewall into the good stuff."

A low hum he'd barely noticed before stopped, and Kentry turned from where he fiddled at the door. "I got it shut down."

"Cut Avion loose."

"Then what?" Kentry asked as he aimed his laser at the manacles.

"Find a hiding spot by the loading bay and bunk down with Avion until we can safely get him out of here."

"But what about the other cells?"

"Xylo and I will check them out. Avion will be a detriment in his current state and hold us back if we need to exit quickly or engage in battle."

"Aye, sir." Kentry hoisted Avion's sagging frame onto his shoulder. "Should we send new instructions to the crew of the ship?"

"Yes. It's time they came knocking at the front door. I have a feeling, by the time we're done, we're going to need a rapid getaway." And quick access to their medical bay.

"Do you think they outnumber us?"

"Yes, but as we know, that's never a problem when it comes to humans." One cyborg could handle a dozen humans.

"If you're not worried about resistance, then why do we need Aphelion and the ship?"

"Because now I'm pissed." And when Aramus got mad, things had a tendency of blowing up.

Chapter Five

Aramus and Xylo hit two more guarded cells, guns no longer set to stun. Who needed prisoners when they had Avion to answer their questions? Besides, now it wasn't just a rescue mission, but a vengeance one. No one hurt their kind and lived to tell about it. Not with Aramus in charge.

Cell by cell, they explored. Unfortunately, the occupants of those rooms didn't have much left to them. They didn't rouse at all during their rescue, nor were they cyborg. It seemed the humans weren't adverse to experimenting and torturing their own kind, but with what, they couldn't at first discern until they came to the fourth cell. More heavily guarded than the last few, this one had an alarm blare to life when they breached it. The seal on the room broken, gaseous air, high in carbon dioxide, whistled out. Aramus only vaguely wondered at the odd presence of the gas for a moment before he beheld the reason why.

A gray-skinned being lay strapped to a gurney within the room, which had been setup as some sort of medical bay. Machines beeped and whirred while tubes, some dripping fluid, others siphoning blood, entered the body from several points.

"Holy fuck, is that a goddamned ET?" Xylo queried.

His first impulse was to say yes, but the more Aramus stared at the humanoid creature, the more he wondered. What were the chances alien life would so closely resemble their own? "I don't know what it is." Whatever it was, Joe and the others back home would want to know about it.

More alarms went off, monitoring systems that flashed red lights as the thing on the gurney twitched.

"Fuck! Fuck! Fuck!" Aramus cursed as the thing gasped for breath, a breath it couldn't find in the suddenly oxygen-rich environment.

"He's dying," Xylo observed.

"I can see that!" he barked. What to do? He couldn't replace the seals on the door and he saw nothing to give the being the air it so desperately needed.

"Doctor," whispered the pale thin lips of the creature. "Find the doc—" The big orbs, with their large black pupils, blinked once, twice, then shut just as the chest stopped rising.

Damn it! Joe would not be happy he'd let the weird being die. It didn't matter he couldn't have known what hid behind the door. He should have paid more attention. The heavy-duty seals should have warned him.

"What did the alien mean do you think, when it said to find the doctor? Do you think it meant the doctor in charge of this place?"

"How the hell should I know?"

"What are we going to do about this?" Xylo waved his hand at the body.

"We'll have to bring it. Even though it died, Einstein and the others will want to see it." See it, dissect it, and figure out what the fuck it was.

A boom rocked the installation. It seemed Aphelion had gotten the message and was inviting himself in. Good. It would make transporting the corpse easier.

"I want you to take the body to the ship. Place it in a stasis chamber."

"What about you?"

"You heard the thing. I need to find a doctor." And once they got some answers, teach this doctor a lesson, a painful one.

Chapter Six

Aramus met up with the other half of the landing team outside the bay where the *SSBiteMe*'s exterior guns mowed down the small group of mercenaries that stood their ground. As if they could make a dent in his ship.

Kyle had a body slung over his shoulder. "Report."

"We had to kill some humans, sir. They pulled weapons on us and began to fire."

He waved their apology away. "Forget about stunning them. Things have changed. Deadly force is to be used on the soldiers and mercs, but if you find any medical personal, bring them to me alive."

"And if the enemy surrenders?"

It stuck in his craw to say it, but he knew what Joe would do. "If any craven humans give themselves up, then take them prisoner as well."

"Aye, sir."

"What did your team find?" Aramus asked.

Kyle's face twisted. "We discovered this place is fucked up. We located two cyborgs, sir. One died as we were escaping. Fluke head shot by a merc. The other we had to sedate as she went wild when we freed her."

"She?" Aramus queried.

"Yes, sir. We located a female unit. She's been badly damaged though." Kyle indicated the limp body he carried.

"What the fuck were they up to?" Aramus mused aloud.

"Some seriously messed-up shit," one of his crew muttered.

You knew it was bad when even cyborgs were rattled. "Take the female to the ship and then return to continue your search. This place is woefully undermanned considering the extent of their operations, but full of surprises. Have Aphelion hook up our computer and download everything he can."

"Yes, sir."

Orders given, Aramus took a moment to pull up a map on a nearby computer panel, the blinking red lights showing the path of destruction he and his team had left behind them. Only two other branches left.

Aramus stalked off, angry, not just at what he'd found but pissed at Seth too. How had he known about this place? What was this place? What were they doing? For once, Aramus wanted to know more than just who his next target was. He wanted to know why. He needed answers.

Come out, come out wherever you are, Doctor. I want to talk with you.

The next group of soldiers he ran across fired at him, and Aramus let them, the rip of bullets though his flesh feeding the blazing anger within. The blood they shed as he viciously tore into them soothed the burn but did not extinguish it.

No amount of blood or screaming could ever atone for what the humans kept doing. For the pain they kept causing.

Noting the seals on the door his latest mercenary victims had guarded, Aramus left the portal intact, guessing that it contained one of the gray-skinned experiments. He didn't want to risk killing it.

The next two doors he broke down had neither soldiers nor seals to protect them, but anything with a lock merited a peek. Inside, he found humans, medical workers by their white coats. A biologist according to the one who stuttered as he declared his profession. A chemist spat another, a feisty female who demanded he give her a communicator so she could contact her father, some kind of big shot back on earth. He gagged her before tying her up. He had little time or patience for a demanding human female.

One door left. He almost turned away. He'd seen enough of the violence and misery hiding behind the portals. He might dislike humans on principle, but even he drew a line at torture. And that's what it was. These weren't the result of some conditioning exercises such as he and other cyborgs were exposed to. The things he'd seen, the scars and bruises, had nothing to do with making the recipients tougher or testing new hardware. It was done for pure, malicious pleasure. *I might be a violent son of a bitch, but I draw the line at torturing for fun.*

So was it any wonder he hesitated for a fraction of a second before the last door in this tunnel? That he spent a moment wondering what fresh atrocity he might discover?

Get a hold of yourself, soldier. He gave himself a solid mental kick in the ass. Now was not the time to get in touch with his emotions. But, he made a note to deal later with his defective programming that was letting all these unwanted feelings seep out.

The locked door gave easily under the brute force applied to it and swung open to reveal a small cell with a flickering light. As with the other rooms given to the incarcerated humans, it held a small cot, washbasin and toilet, and a single frightened occupant.

The huddled form peeked up, knees tucked to the chest under a stained white gown, a tangle of hair covering the dirty face. Big eyes stared at him, and Aramus almost took a step back, not out of fear but because of the resignation in the eyes. She expected to die. The gun in his hand lowered. This abused human posed no danger to him.

"Who are you?" he barked. Not cyborg, that was for sure. Of that he'd have wagered his right hand on. If wrong, he could always replace it with a new mechanical one sporting the latest in clip-on weaponry and projectile fingertips.

The recoil at his sharp question made him almost regret his tone. But humans, abused or not, didn't deserve his pity.

"I'm—I'm—" The dulcet whisper placed her in the female category. The stutter placed her in his trying-my-patience one as well.

"I don't have all day. Who are you?"

"I'm Riley Carmichael."

"What are you doing here? Are you a doctor?"

"I guess you would call me a doctor."

"So you're a doctor?"

"Of sorts."

But was she the one the dead gray thing wanted him to find? This tiny slip of a human, this pathetic dirty thing, couldn't be the cause of the torture he'd seen. But, then again, appearances could be deceiving. Except in his case. He looked like a big, bad motherfucker, and he was. Times ten. "Come with me."

"Are you here to rescue us?" Fear faded in the big blue eyes as hope brightened her gaze.

"You could say that."

Standing, she barely reached his chin, and her wrists felt brittle when he gripped them to lash them behind her back with a zip tie.

"What are you doing?" She peered up at him, the sharp scent of her fear acrid and displeasing.

"Securing you."

"But I thought you were here to rescue me and the others."

"I'm here to rescue victims."

"And you don't consider me a victim?" She sounded astonished.

"You're human. Other than a few bruises, and some dirt, you don't seem abused."

"They kept me locked in a cell. Beat me if I didn't obey. Starved me half to death to keep me weak. How much more abused do you want me to be?"

"Are you able to speak? Are you chained to a wall? Did they experiment on you?" He bombarded her with questions, each one causing her to recoil as if slapped.

"No, but only because they needed me."

"Lucky for you, I also need you for the moment, or you would be joining the other humans in death. Now shut up, or I will gag you as I did the other female."

The threat clamped her lips shut, and silent, she preceded him from the cell, her step hesitant, her head swinging from left to right as she took in the carnage outside her confinement. He heard her swallow hard as she stepped gingerly over a cooling puddle of blood.

Before he could contact his crew and get the latest update, a cadre of soldiers, military by their bearing and dress, came jogging around the corner. Aramus braced for the bullets sure to follow but quickly frowned as one of them yelled, "There she is. Shoot her."

Her? Shouldn't he be their target? How rude.

The female in question didn't dive back into the cell—which was the smartest move—or freeze in place—which would have guaranteed her death. Nope, instead she showed a modicum of intelligence as she hid behind him with a squeaked, "Don't just stand there. Kill them before they kill us!"

With pleasure.

Aramus let his knife fly, the blade hitting one of the soldiers preparing to fire in the neck. Blood spurted. Not an instant death, but a fatal blow nonetheless. The rest got to experience firsthand the accuracy of a cyborg trained to never miss. While their bullets sprayed all over the place, Aramus picked them off, barely flinching as the occasional lucky shot struck him. As for the guy who'd ordered the doctor's death?

He stalked after him when he would have turned tail and run. Tripping over the bodies of his dead squad, the human blubbered for mercy.

"Don't kill me. I was just following orders."

"Whose orders?"

It seemed he wouldn't find out as the soldier suddenly went rigid, his eyes rolling back in his head until only the whites appeared. As his body thrashed, foam began to spill from his mouth. Aramus dropped the body in disgust. It seemed the military didn't want them getting their hands on their soldiers.

A soft touch against his back had him whirling, ready to fire. He held back at the last moment as he realized the petite doctor had crept up to him. She peered around his frame and murmured. "Strychnine, or some variation of. Often the main ingredient of suicide pills."

"Fucking fanatics."

"At least he's dead."

"Without answering any questions. Why did they want to terminate you?"

"I'd say that was obvious. So I wouldn't talk to you."

"Are there many more soldiers?"

She shrugged. "I wouldn't know. I was kept locked up for the most part."

"What do you know?"

"That I'm glad they're dead. Thank you."

He grunted in reply. He didn't want her gratitude. "Why did you hide behind me instead of running away?"

"Run to where? If you ask me, sticking to you seems like the smartest way of getting out of here."

Good point. Would wonders never cease? He'd finally found a human with an ounce of common sense.

Aramus used his internal communicator to check in with his team.

Status report.

Only one room left to clear in the southwest corridor, announced Kyle. *We are no longer encountering resistance. However, the remaining prison cells are either empty or have bodies. It seems the soldiers are executing the inhabitants, staff and prisoners, before deserting their posts.*

Less deserted than fled, Aphelion announced grimly. *My sensors picked up a vessel leaving the atmosphere.*

And you didn't give chase? Aramus queried.

My calculations, given their speed, vessel capabilities, and trajectory, put my chances of capturing them at less than seventeen percent, so I chose to remain here as an additional means of support.

It galled him to have lost some of the assholes running this place, but Aphelion had made the right choice. Given the injured cyborgs they'd recovered and the fact they needed to sweep the base for clues before departing, or the humans arrived to clean it up—AKA via nuke—their current mission took precedence over a futile chase. *How many cyborgs did we liberate?*

Two males, one female in total. Another pair died during the raid, both of whom were female.

What about those gray beings? Other than the dead one, how many live ones are left?

All of the aliens have disappeared, including the dead one.

Aramus didn't bother correcting Aphelion about the alien comment. It seemed an apt description for the moment given they didn't know who and what those gray-skinned beings were.

What do you mean disappeared?

When the units returned to those cells to recover the body and to see if there was a means of transporting the other two, we discovered all three rooms empty.

Fuck! I wanted to bring at least one of them back for Einstein to study.

The good news is we did recover a few humans before the soldiers could kill them. Hopefully, they will be able to fill in some of the blanks and let us know what was going on. The bad news is they were all civilians. The soldiers that were left tied up and unconscious are gone, or dead.

Suicide? Not unheard of with fanatic troops, and he'd seen one resort to it already.

Not unless they managed bullet holes in their heads with their hands still tied.

Someone didn't want to leave witnesses behind. *So what do we have in total for live bodies?*

Five humans in total. Two are mute, another is gravely injured, but the other two seem intact.

Make that six. I've got one of the doctors with me, Aramus added, frowning down at the little female who remained tucked close enough he'd need a pry bar to remove her.

What would you like me to do with them?

Place them in our holding room. I'll be by to question them later. How is the download of their computers going?

Slowly. Someone began a wipe not long after they discovered we'd infiltrated. I managed to save some bits and pieces. Hopefully Einstein can make some sense of it. I've got Kentry yanking out drives as we speak in case Einstein can restore the information.

Try to make it quick. We have no idea if the ship that escaped is going to return with friends. We might have taken them by surprise with our ambush, but we're not equipped to take on a fleet of attack cruisers.

Understood.

Excellent. I'll be coming aboard shortly with my human prisoner.

Marching the doctor up the gangplank, Aramus found she didn't require any added incentive to keep her moving—she remained glued to his side—but she also didn't remain silent.

"Who are you?"

He didn't answer. She wasn't deterred.

"Is this your ship? Where are you taking me?"

"I'm going to take you back to your cell if you don't shut up," he finally growled.

He immediately regretted his harsh tone as her thin shoulders rolled in, making her petite frame even more compact, as if she braced for a blow. For some strange reason, a part of him wanted to offer reassurance.

Reminding himself she was a human and not deserving of pity didn't help. Damned human emotion frailties. They sought to overcome his common sense. He'd reboot himself the first chance he got and cleanse himself of the defective feelings that threatened.

I will not let my weaker, human side win. I am cyborg. Logic is all that matters.

Chapter Seven

Riley didn't know what to think. On the one hand, when the imposing figure dressed head to toe in space gear had shown up at her cell door, kicking his way in like some movie action hero, she'd felt such fear then hope as he stated his intention to rescue. Then he'd made it clear with his tone and words that he didn't consider her a victim, but a prisoner. And the way he spoke of her, as if they weren't from the same species…

She sneaked peeks at him as they strode up the violence-splattered hallway to the loading bay. With the environmental suit he wore, she could discern very little about her rescuer other than the fact he bore a human shape. Then again, the mutant bodies she'd examined were also bipedal.

Was this a rescue party for the poor experiments? Had she gotten flung from one untenable situation to another? *Oh god, I hope they're not going to run tests on me like they were doing on the corpses I examined.* Given what she'd seen during the past few months, she wouldn't blame them if they felt a need for retaliation, but how to make them understand she was just as much a victim? Would they even care?

A hole blasted in the bay doors showcased another of the suited rescuers standing guard. To preserve the pressure and integrity of the installation—a fact she appreciated—a sealed tunnel had been suctioned to the hole leading onto a very military spacecraft.

"Are you from earth?" she asked, forgetting his order to remain silent.

The big being didn't reprimand her, but his reply didn't really answer her question. "Not anymore."

What was that supposed to mean? "So you're human?"

"Nope."

"Alien?"

"Most definitely not!" Before she could query further, he growled, "Zip it."

She clamped her lips shut. No use provoking him. Not until she knew more about the situation.

Marched into a barren room, if she ignored the huddled forms of other prisoners, she jumped when the door behind her slid shut with an ominous clang. Bolts slid shut, locking her in.

Great. I exchanged one prison for another.

Straightening her spine, she decided not to let herself despair. They obviously didn't intend to kill her, or the big fellow would have done so already. *But he could be saving me for some torture later.*

Yeah, she wouldn't let her mind stray in that direction. Not yet. She needed to stick to the positive if she wanted to stay sane. *So what do I have going for me?*

One, she was alive with all her body parts intact.

Two, he'd not actually harmed her. While he'd tied her arms behind her, he'd done so just enough to keep her from acting out.

Three, she was out of her cell and hopefully getting off this godforsaken planet.

Four, the unknown meant hope.

Five...

Was it her, or did she hear ominous hissing? Up went her gaze and she forgot about listing the positives about her new situation because, sure enough, a white gas oozed from the ventilation grills.

"We're g-g-g-oing to d-d-d-ie," moaned one of the other occupants.

"Oh shut up, Percy. It's a decontamination cloud. You can tell by the smell."

"D-d-don't tell me to shut up!" The fellow named Percy shot a glare at the woman who'd rebuked him, his index finger pushing up his thick glasses.

"Then don't be such a whiny baby. Or would you prefer to be back in your cell?"

"You were prisoners too?" Riley ventured.

"We all were. It seems our captors aren't interested in the soldiers." A fine mist enveloped them, the scent acrid and vinegary. It tingled on the skin. Holding out her arm, the pretty Latina pursed her full lips as she glared at the gas. She bore red marks around her mouth as if something had recently covered it. "Would it have killed them to give us a shower?" she grumbled. "I am so sick of smelling like a locker room."

A shower would be nice, one without a guard leering, with warm water and actual soap. Funny how the small things Riley used to take for granted seemed like such luxuries now.

Taking a closer peek at the group, Riley realized she only recognized one other person, David something or other. He'd sometimes been a silent presence during the autopsies, taking blood and tissue samples. He lay prone on the floor, a bandage stained in red covering his midsection.

"Who are you?" asked the woman. "I'm Carmen."

"Riley."

Carmen pointed to the male wearing glasses. "And that stuttering idiot is Percy."

"I-I'm not an id-diot," he stammered. "Bitch."

Carmen blew Percy a kiss while he scowled. It seemed they knew each other but didn't necessarily like one another.

"Anyone know where we are?" Riley asked, straying closer to the Latina, who seemed to have the best handle on things.

"Some kind of military ship."

"So the federation has us?"

"Ha. Like hell. Did you see the suits those guys were wearing? Nope. My guess is pirates or cyborgs."

"Cyborgs!" Riley recoiled from the word. Of all the options, that one scared her the most. Everyone knew how much the cyborgs hated humans. How their programming had failed and they'd turned into killing machines, murdering anything with a pulse.

"Don't tell me you believe that hyped-up mumbo jumbo the newsfeeds have been spouting?"

Riley shifted her weight from foot to foot as Carmen stared at her, disdain curling her lip. "I saw the footage of the chaos they leave behind when a colony is invaded."

"Chaos, yes. Done by them? No." Carmen motioned for her to turn around. Riley wondered why for only a moment before the fetters around her wrists fell to the floor.

"Where did you get the knife?"

"I had it on me when they captured me. None of them bothered to search us. I guess they don't see us as a threat."

Eyeing the two females sitting on the floor staring into space, the unconscious male prone on the floor, Percy who kept wringing his hands, and Carmen, who tucked the knife away to finger comb her hair, Riley could kind of see why.

"So what do they see in us?" Riley asked. If they weren't here to save them, then why had they taken them prisoner?

Carmen shrugged. "Hopefully not parts."

"What!"

"Just kidding. That's another rumor falsely circulated to get you all freaking. My guess is they're looking for answers."

"Aren't we all?" muttered Riley.

"M-Maybe they want to know about the aliens."

"They're not aliens," Carmen stated.

"Are we talking about the gray ones?"

"What else? Did you get to see them?" Carmen's attention focused on Riley.

"Yeah."

"And what did you think? What were they? Did any of them talk to you?"

Riley's nose wrinkled. "Dead bodies don't say much."

"What are you, a coroner?"

"Forensic anthropologist. I study corpses."

"So you should know then. Were they alien or human?"

"Neither and both. It's almost as if they mashed some foreign DNA with human. You obviously dealt with them, what was your take?"

"I was hired as a psychologist. My task was to get them to communicate."

"And?"

"They didn't have much to say. I mean, they spoke English for the most part, but most of our conversations were along the lines of 'Help me', 'Kill me', or 'I'm going to kill you'. Then there was the one guy who kept saying he wanted to fuck me, but I don't know if he was part of the same project because he was the only one they didn't keep in a gas chamber. Actually, I'm fairly certain he was cyborg."

"They had cyborgs too? I didn't see the bodies of any."

"Maybe because they didn't die like the others. They're tough sons of bitches."

*

Tough indeed. Aramus had tuned in to listen to the prisoners, seeing what he could glean before he began his questioning. The installation was secure. The only living beings left were the cyborgs performing sweeps and the rats, which seemed to follow humans no matter where they went in the galaxy.

By all indications, the prisoners they'd acquired weren't major players for the faceless company who seemed to constantly stay one step ahead of them. However, they had information, answers to some of the questions plaguing him.

"What are we going to do with them?" Aphelion asked.

Aramus muted the live feed and drummed his fingers on the armrest of his seat. "Kill them."

"Even I know you're not seriously contemplating that."

No. He wasn't. Human or not, they seemed to be victims, not perpetrators. "I guess we question them."

"And then?"

Then…what? They couldn't just put them back where they found them. The installation was compromised, and once they unsealed their ship from the hole they'd made, the planet would reclaim the mountain. Dropping them off on earth, also not a possibility. So what did that leave? Not much.

"Termination would be most efficient." Even if he lacked the enthusiasm to mete out such an extreme to a group that obviously didn't deserve further punishment.

"Why did I know you were going to say that?" Aphelion shook his head in clear disgust. "Why must everything with you end in death? There's got to be another option."

"I guess we could dump them on a colony planet and let the settlers deal with them."

"Won't the company go after them?"

"Only if they know they're there."

"Which will happen within an hour of their arrival as soon as the first notification is sent back to earth. It's a death sentence not only to them but the colony who gets them."

Aramus scowled. "What the hell else am I supposed to do with them? I can't kill them. I can't drop them off. What do you suggest then?"

"We could keep them."

"Keep? Are you out of your fucking mind?"

"My mind is quite intact and functioning at a ninety-eight-point-three percent efficiency."

"I'd run a diagnostic to be sure, because your suggestion is highly illogical."

"Why?"

"Because."

"Because is not an acceptable answer."

If ever there was a time Aramus hated cyborg logic, now was that time. "Because we can't have a gaggle of humans running around my ship causing trouble, that's why."

"So we keep them confined until we get back home and let Joe deal with them. They wouldn't be the first humans brought back for the good of our society."

True. Despite the general dislike for humans, or the ones who'd done them wrong at any rate, some of his brethren didn't mind them. Heck, some of his brothers even took humans as cohabiting partners. They even had humans working amongst them. But they'd been taken from harsh punishing environments where earth politicians had dumped them. The cyborgs came along and gave these society rejects a second chance to live as free men and women with rights.

The prisoners he'd just picked up though? They worked for the enemy. They'd abetted the torture and experimentation of cyborgs and others. How could he and his crew knowingly bring them into the fold? What if one or more of them were spies?

"What if they're lying? What if their apparent abuse is a ruse to get us to let down our guard, allowing them to infiltrate and send back information to their superiors?"

"I think I'm not the one who needs to run a diagnostic. You are letting paranoia control you."

"It's called caution."

"Semantics. You can't live suspecting every human you meet is out to get you."

"Why not? It's kept me alive."

"And miserable."

"Says you. I am perfectly content. I am the commander of this ship. I get to travel. Explore. Bring back goods for the cyborg colony." Kill humans who got in his way. What more could a cyborg ask for?

An end to the emptiness inside me that plagues me whenever I am alone. But that, he kept to himself.

Chapter Eight

One by one, Aramus had the prisoners taken to be bathed, dressed, and then brought in for questioning. With the exception of the mute women, and the still comatose male, they all told varying shades of the same story. They were lured with promises of a great job that required utmost discretion. Once segregated from their friends and family, they found themselves whisked to destinations unknown where they were forced to work, under abusive conditions. Where their tales differed was in their specialties.

The male with the irritating speech impediment named Percy was a biologist. He took and reviewed tissue and bodily fluid samples. Problem was, while he'd gotten a first-hand look at the before and after results of the experiments, speaking with him left Aramus irritated. He decided to leave the questioning of him to Einstein and Joe, especially once he realized the male knew nothing about the cyborgs being held prisoner.

The female, Carmen, a psychologist, proved more interesting.

She entered with a flip of her hair and a defiant expression. Seating herself before him, she made a show of crossing her legs and leaning in such a way as to put her décolletage on display. As if her feeble attempt at seduction would distract Aramus from doing his job.

They went through the basics. Name, occupation, her interactions with the prisoners. She answered without hesitation, and even when told she was on board a cyborg vessel, her demeanor remained unchanged, unlike Percy who had sweated and stammered even harder at the news.

"You say you spoke with one who might have been a cyborg?" Aramus leaned back in his chair and fixed her with a stare.

She lifted one shoulder in a shrug. "Maybe. He wasn't like the others, that's for sure. He was a lot cockier for one, as if unworried by the fact he was a prisoner."

"Did he give you a name?"

A shake of her head implied no. "I asked, but he just smiled and said if I wanted to know I'd have to give him something in return."

"As in?"

"What does any man want of an attractive woman?"

No coyness here. "So you refused to have sex?"

"I wasn't given the opportunity. After that session, I never saw him again."

"Is this the male you spoke to?" Aramus called up an image of Avion before the torture that left him so scarred.

She shook her head. "No. The one I spoke with had dark skin and eyes. I'd wager he was mulatto or Puerto Rican."

An unknown then, as Aramus's databanks showed no cyborg with those characteristics either missing or presumed dead. They spent some more time, going back and forth, him fishing for answers, her answering seemingly without guile, all the while flirting. In the end, though, she knew nothing of import. "That's all for now. You may leave."

"Are you sure you want me to?" Carmen leaned forward, far enough that her breasts practically fell out of her jumpsuit. "It must be lonely out here in space. I noticed a definite lack of women."

"Because females are disruptive to missions."

"Not all of us. Some of us would be happy to stay out of the way until we're *needed*." A lick of her lips completed her less-than-subtle invitation.

A moue of distaste twisted his lips. "No thanks. Unlike human males, we control our bodies, and the mission always comes first."

"If you change your mind, you know where to find me." With a glance meant to be sultry thrown over her shoulder, the brazen female left with swish of her hips.

She's trouble, that one. With a capital T. While Aramus found it easy to ignore her overtures, he couldn't deny others might find her and her offer appealing. Not everyone had his iron control when it came to keeping their lust in check.

Cyborgs were a lot of things, strong, fast, enhanced, and lusty. Very lusty, especially once the military programming controlling their every move was eradicated. It seemed good soldiers needed testosterone, lots of it, so while certain parts of them were replaced when they got changed from human to cyborg, the things that gave them their edge, like cock and balls, remained intact. And very functional.

For a logical society, even Aramus couldn't deny they were a horny bunch. Cybernetic units liked to fuck. A lot. It was why they kept a standing arrangement with a few space brothels. It kept the fighting amongst units down. But there was no whorehouse in this section of space he could travel to, which meant Carmen and her flirtation would probably find takers. He could already predict the trouble that would cause, especially if she didn't restrict her sexual favors to a single male.

I hope I don't end up having to smash a few heads together. Then again, he could always use some exercise.

But enough of that. He'd deal with that problem once it cropped up. Back to his current task. Questioning the prisoners. He called the last one in, the petite female he'd rescued and whose hopeful stare had remained with him long after he'd dropped her off.

Why her gaze stuck with him, he couldn't have said. He'd not found anything particularly extraordinary about her other than her diminutive height. Such shortness seemed defective to him. Then again, he'd noted in the case of at least two of the female cyborgs they'd rescued in the past that those in charge of the cyborg project seemed to prefer experimenting on smaller females.

But the prisoner is not cyborg. She was a human, or so the scans indicated. A human doctor who'd willingly, or not, possibly experimented on his kind and the mutated beings they'd yet to decipher.

He didn't immediately look up when the door to his private chamber slid open, occupied with glancing over the last radar reports that showed no activity in the area. Then again, as they well knew, their technology wasn't always reliable when it came to seeing what was truly out there.

"Um, hello?" Her hesitant query brought his gaze up and the sharp retort to quiet until he was ready, died on his lips as he beheld her.

What had happened to the dirty waif he'd rescued? The woman he'd saved stood before him, and he couldn't help but stare. Her shoulder-length hair brown hair shone in the fluorescent lights, the ends uneven and curling slightly with dampness. Scrubbed clean, her skin exhibited an even creamy tone, except for her cheeks, which pinked as he continued to eyeball her. He couldn't help himself, especially when he noted how the jumpsuit they'd given her hugged voluptuous curves not meant for the slim outfit, making the cleavage that strained at the front enclosure more pronounced. A lick of her full lips caused the most surprising chain reaction because, during that momentary peek of the tip of her tongue, he couldn't help imagining sliding his mouth along those plump lips, sucking on them, and this vivid visualization caused him to harden in a most unforeseen manner.

Stand down. He ordered his cock to behave. And it did, mostly. Drumming his fingertips on his desk, he glared at her. Undaunted, she stared right back, her gaze flicking to the top of his head.

"Oh my god," she whispered. "You are a cyborg."

For some reason her observation stung. "Of course I am. What else did you think I was?"

The coloration in her cheeks deepened. "I wasn't sure. When you rescued me you had on a space suit so I couldn't see your face, and it's not as if you introduced yourself."

Her well-reasoned answer still didn't ease the sting at the way she'd reacted to the discovery of what he was. Then again, what did he care what one human thought? "I did not realize that introductions were necessary. Perhaps the next time I save your ass I should wear a sign saying, I am a cyborg."

"There's no reason to be rude."

"I was being sarcastic."

"I didn't know cyborgs could do that."

"Do what? Wield the English language?"

"No, make jests."

Sarcasm wasn't making fun. It was a way of expressing himself. "I do not joke."

"If you say so. What happened to your head?"

Blunt, but as a male who didn't like to pussyfoot, he couldn't disparage her directness. He could however fuck with her. "It's partially metal."

"I can see that, but why? I've seen cyborgs before, not in person of course, but on the newsfeeds, and while some have sported mechanical legs and arms, I've never seen one with a—"

"Metal skull? It was a present from a woman." His first meeting with a female cyborg did not go well. She'd shot him, obeying a buried command given to her by the military. Lucky for him, she had bad aim—or as Seth claimed, he'd used up the horseshoe stored in his ass—and he'd survived. Half of his head didn't. He rather preferred his new bald pate and metallic crown. He felt it enhanced his cyborg appearance. And gave him better reception.

The female's eyes widened. "Someone shot you in the head?"

She seemed genuinely appalled. As if a mere human cared. He didn't believe her act for a moment. "Among other places. I've also been shot in the torso, back, arms, legs. Most didn't leave lasting scars, as my nanos healed the damage."

"You sound so nonchalant about it."

"Because it's a fact of life for cyborgs. It's why we were created. To take as much damage as possible and still keep fighting." Him, bitter? Always.

"Did they hurt?" Again, her concern and curiosity seemed authentic.

"Only the first few times. Then you learn to shut off the pain and move faster." Not to mention improve your aim so that the bastards shooting died before they did something irreparable. Cyborgs could sustain a lot of damage, but nanotechnology could only heal so much. And why exactly was he answering her questions anyway? He was the one in charge here, not her. He was the one who needed answers—not pity. "As if you give a shit. You can stop pretending."

"Who says I'm pretending? You were shot. Numerous times by your account. I'd have to be inhuman not to feel something."

"Or cyborg."

"So it's true what they say? You don't feel emotions?"

"Oh, we feel. Right now, I feel annoyed, violent, and a tad bit hungry. Military rations really aren't fit for anyone."

The ghost of a smile on her lips at his slip of tongue irritated him more than his unexpected jest. Irritated, because he wondered what a full smile would look like on her face. *Get your mind back on task, soldier.* Her facial expressions were not a concern. What she did for the military or the corporation, though, was.

Pulling up her file, he concentrated on the contents he'd downloaded to his BCI earlier. It was incomplete, given the damage done to the records by the hard drive wipes. He began his questioning by confirming the basics. "Your name is Riley Carmichael."

"Yes. And you are?"

"Asking the questions."

"And again being rude."

He glanced up from his summarized report. For some reason it didn't please him when she wouldn't hold his stern glare. "I am not your friend."

"I'd say that was obvious."

Did she sulk? Her tone seemed to indicate she did. He chose to ignore it. "You are twenty-seven years old. Single. A paltry five foot one, one hundred and forty-five pounds."

"What do you know, all that starving paid off."

He ignored her and continued. "You have a degree in forensic anthropology. Did an internship at a morgue. Attended—"

"Yes, yes and yes. Does any of this really matter?"

"Facts are important."

"To you, maybe. I'm more interested in other things, such as why have you taken me prisoner?"

Every time he thought he had her pegged as weak and timid, she surprised him by speaking out. He found he preferred her small bouts of courage to her hunching when he scowled at her too long.

"I took you prisoner because you are the enemy."

"Enemy?" She uttered a short laugh. Peering down at herself, she gestured to her body, something he refused to look at—the size of her breasts and hips not necessary for this interrogation—before returning her gaze to him. "Exactly how am I a danger to you?"

Because, even though he kept his gaze on her face, she made his cock stir when it should remain dormant. He ground the heel of his palm into it, to no effect. "You are human."

"And so are you."

Thanks for the reminder. He grimaced. "Not anymore."

"But you began that way. Surely the machines they melded you with haven't completely eradicated who you are, or were?"

"No, the military, with help of the company, did that with their training."

Her brow creased. "I don't understand."

"Like hell you don't. You worked for them. You saw how they treated us. Or are you going to pretend you never saw the cyborgs being kept captive?"

"The only thing I ever saw were bodies and my jailors."

"So you deny involvement in the cyborg project?"

"Deny? Of course I am. You're the first cyborg I've ever met."

"Bullshit."

"It's the truth."

"The facility we pulled you from had several cyborgs incarcerated. Are you telling me they never had you examine one?"

"I think I'd kind of remember." Now it was she wielding the sarcasm. As the recipient, he didn't care for it.

"So what bodies did you see?"

"Lots of mutated human ones."

"Are you sure they were human?"

She huddled in on herself. "Yes, at least they were before the experiments."

His attention, which attempted to stray from her lips lower to a shadowy décolletage, sharpened and returned to her face. "Explain."

She fidgeted. "I don't know what they were doing, but I saw the results. Ever watch mutant movies where mad scientists try to blend animals with humans and end up with monsters?"

"No." But he'd seen the result of man mixing human with machine.

"Oh. Well, imagine if you can a body that's had its DNA reprogrammed."

"Like I've never fucking seen or heard of that before." He rolled his eyes and then almost smacked himself at his human reaction. *Get a fucking grip, soldier!*

She blushed. "Sorry. I forgot for a moment who I was speaking with."

As if.

"Anyway, as I was saying, the bodies they brought to me were deformed."

"Deformed how?"

"Thicker body mass. Enlarged organs, and in some cases duplicates. Extra ribs. Thicker bone growth. Fused in some cases with others. The actual density and composition was changed. And then there were things growing from the body. Protrusions from the spine for the most part, skull too at times. Elongated teeth. Grayish skin tones. Longer fingers, but only on some of them."

Aramus frowned. "And these weren't birth defects?"

"No. At least I don't think so. Neither were they grafts."

"Did your employers say what caused them?"

"I tried asking once." Her gaze dropped to her lap where her fingers knotted with each other.

Even he recognized fear when he saw it. "And?"

"I woke up three days later with a broken jaw, bruised ribs, and a healthy respect for silence."

A sudden rage filled him. Who would dare beat this tiny, defenseless female for daring to ask a reasonable question? The same people who had no problem taking a simple soldier involuntarily drafted and turning him into a fighting machine.

"In your opinion, what were they trying to do?"

"Other than play God?"

"There is no god." He'd studied the Bible, done his research, and arrived at this conclusion because there just wasn't any concrete proof. How so many could believe in an entity no one had ever seen or touched, he didn't understand.

Again, she surprised him. "On that we agree. But they certainly wanted to set themselves up as creators. However, you asked what I thought they'd been trying to do. Given what I saw during the autopsies, I'd say they were trying to inject humans with foreign DNA."

"Foreign as in…"

"This is going to sound crazy, but I think they were using some kind of alien DNA."

Why did it seem like everywhere he turned, someone was trying to cram evidence of ET's down his throat? "Do you have any proof?"

"No."

"Then I don't understand how you can jump to that conclusion."

She fluttered her hands and blew out a breath. "Call it instinct. Something about the organs of the affected bodies just doesn't seem right. Certain characteristics kept repeating and are unlike anything I've ever run across. If you did a DNA comparison, you'd probably know for sure."

Aramus made a mental note to re-question Percy. Given he was in charge of collecting and testing samples, he should know and had either misled or withheld that information from Aramus. *Not for long. I have ways of making him talk.*

"How did you end up working for the company?" Aramus had no logical reason to ask, other than a curiosity to know what would lead a woman such as herself to agree to work for such a vile group.

"They came to me and lied. Said they had a great opportunity to study medical breakthroughs. The money and benefits they quoted were a dream come true. I jumped on the chance."

"They bought you."

"I didn't know when I signed on what they were up to, or I would have never agreed."

"So you claim."

She puffed up with indignation. "Believe me or not. It's the truth. What about you? What were your reasons for volunteering for the cyborg project?"

"Volunteer?" At that he laughed. "None of us ever volunteered. One day we went to sleep as normal men and women, and the next we woke as machines."

"You mean they did this to you without permission?"

"Are you really so naïve to think anyone would volunteer for this?"

"But the media says—"

"A lot of things. Haven't you learned by now most of them aren't true?" His smile mocked her.

Instead of fighting back with more words, her shoulders slumped. "I'm realizing more and more just how dumb I was."

He ordered his tongue to not say the words, *you're not dumb, just too trusting.* He didn't owe this female reassurance. She was just like all the other mindless humans on earth, believing what the media, military, and corporations spoon-fed them.

"That's all for now. A unit will return you to your quarters until we have need of you again." *Say later tonight in my room wearing nothing.* Aramus shoved the unworthy thought away.

"You mean my cell? What are you planning to do with me and the others?"

There was the feisty woman he preferred to see. It made it easy to be himself. "None of your damned business."

"It is my business. I have a right to know."

Impertinently asked, he should have voiced his usual reply, "Death once you're no use to me." Instead, he said, "Why don't you fear me?"

"Why would I?" She met his gaze and held it despite the slight tremor in her frame.

"I am cyborg."

"And?"

"And I hate humans."

"All of us? That seems rather illogical. Only a fraction of humans, by your own admission, are to blame for what happened to you."

How fascinating. She thought to use his own need for logic against him. "You have seen the media reports. We are bloodthirsty monsters. We live to kill."

"As you pointed out, the media doesn't always get its facts straight."

"Oh, they are right about certain things. We have killed. Myself, I've murdered without compunction. Countless gallons of human blood have stained my hands, and yet you have the balls to question me."

"I don't think I've grown a hairy set of balls since my imprisonment," she quipped with a shy smile that jolted him. "Yes, I'll admit I was fooled by the reports I heard. But I'm not stupid. It doesn't take a genius to realize that perhaps the media reports have been grossly exaggerated."

"Did you not see the installation? We killed those running it. Slaughtered them." Why he felt a need to shove this fact in her face he couldn't have said. Did he want her to fear him?

"I saw, and maybe this makes me a monster, but I'm glad. Those mercenaries and doctors running the place weren't human. They deserved what they got. I'm glad they're dead."

Damn her for raising her in his estimation with those vehemently said words. "I could kill you right now and feel no remorse."

"Yet you won't."

"Says who? No one would stop me."

"You won't do it."

"What makes you say that?"

Her blue eyes met his, unwavering before his glower. "You're not a monster."

Four simple words, and yet they struck the heart of him better than a well-aimed bullet. If he'd been standing, he would have staggered. *Fuck me, but she's dangerous.* He needed to put her in her place, but short of snapping her neck, which he couldn't do—for practical reasons because he might still need to question her—he needed to make her understand he wasn't her friend. That he was a force to be reckoned with, a cyborg to be feared. What could he do to this female that wouldn't damage her and would make her eye him differently?

He blamed his malfunctioning cock for what he did next. And for those who wondered, he beat it soundly for its actions—later…while reliving the kiss.

Chapter Nine

One minute, the daunting cyborg sat in his chair, trying to convince her he was a monster. The next, he'd dragged her onto his desk and kissed her.

Surprised by his rapid action, it took Riley a moment to process it. Her body, however, immediately enjoyed it. Despite the situation, she'd found herself attracted to the cyborg the moment she'd stepped into his space.

Sure, he appeared intimidating. What man wouldn't? Towering about six and a half feet with muscles a steroid user would envy and a gruff attitude to put any prison warden to shame. Yet, the more they spoke, him trying to shock her with his bluntness and violent outlook, the more she saw the man within. A male who'd been dealt a harsh hand, who didn't trust, who dealt with situations the only way he knew how—with violence. And yet, this cyborg, this man who wanted her to see him as a brutal killer, had saved her and the others, treating them with more respect than the so-called humans he reviled.

He was no more a monster than she was and nothing like the media would have her believe. *I can't believe I bought into their propaganda.*

He was also ridiculously sexy. Sure, he didn't have the pampered looks of a supermodel, but he was attractive in his own right, his craggy features so masculine, so riveting. His piercing stare had taken in her appearance and strayed to her breasts more than once in obvious male appreciation and yet not once had he made a sexual remark or innuendo.

Which was why his kiss surprised her so much. A part of her understood he did this to shock her, to put her in her place and fear him. It had the opposite effect. Instead, as soon as their lips touched, an almost electrical sensation went through her, a tingle that heated her blood and softened her mouth so that what started as a bruising embrace turned into a sensual exploration of lips, and then the melding of tongues.

It had been so long since she'd enjoyed the touch of a man, or at least a touch not meant to cause pain. Longer still since she'd kissed anyone, her last boyfriend so long ago she scarcely could recall his face. She gave herself to the kiss wholeheartedly, blossoming under the tender caress like a desert bloom after a sudden rain shower. Her body heated, moisture pooling between her thighs, her nipples tightening in anticipation. Even her toes curled as her whole body—

How far would it have gone had the onboard speaker not crackled to life with a static message of, "Avion has woken."

Despite the interruption, he didn't shove her away or end the kiss abruptly. With obvious reluctance, he gave her lower lip a last suck before leaning away from her. What he saw when he stared at her she would have dearly loved to know.

Whatever it was, he didn't like it because his face went from that of bemused kisser to hardened soldier in an instant. "Get the fuck out of here." When she hesitated, he barked, "Now!"

Away she scooted, the portal to the room whisking open as she neared it allowing her to exit. She ran into the solid chest of the cyborg waiting outside. Or at least she assumed he was cyborg. Nothing about his outward appearance, other than his extreme size and fitness, made him seem inhuman.

"Sorry," she muttered, eyes downcast, flustered at what had just occurred.

Her guard didn't seem to notice her frazzled state because he pivoted on his heel with a blandly spoken, "Follow me."

She almost had to run to keep up with the male's longer stride, but she didn't let that stop her from asking questions, anything to get her mind off the surprise kiss. "Are you a cyborg too?"

The guard pivoted his head, more than a normal spine could have handled, to shoot her an amused look. "What do you think?"

"That you should have auditioned for a part in *The Exorcist*."

A crease marred the smoothness of his forehead. "I don't understand the reference."

"Sorry. I was referring to a movie I saw as a teenager."

"One of those entertainment pieces you humans enjoy so much?"

How odd the way he spoke, as if they were two different species. Did cyborgs truly see themselves as so different? *They started out human.* And definitely kissed like one. Maybe better. Yet, they seemed to equate themselves to something on a whole different plane. Did they truly not recall their time when they lived normal lives on earth? She realized her guide was waiting for a reply. "Yes, that's what I'm referring to. Don't you watch them too?"

"No. They have no educational value."

"They're not meant to teach but pass the time."

"I'd rather spend my time being constructive."

"All work, no play? That doesn't seem like much fun."

"Fun is not a system requirement. We have arrived at your quarters. Food will be delivered shortly. Please inform the others."

He didn't quite shove her through the opening, but the cyborg, who didn't think he needed fun in his life, couldn't get rid of her fast enough.

Before she could dwell on their odd way of viewing things—or the incredible kiss—she was bombarded by questions.

"What did they do to you?"

"What d-d-d-o they want?"

"Are we going home?"

"Are they going to k-k-kill us?"

Riley held up a hand. "Whoa. One at a time."

Carmen, as usual, made sure she got the first question in. "Did you find out what their plans for us are?"

"The guy I was speaking to didn't say. He seemed to want to know what we were up to at the installation."

"Did you tell him?"

"I did. I saw no point in holding back."

"But they're c-c-yborgs."

"Who have treated us more kindly than our employers."

"For now." Percy peered at the camera that recorded their every move and speech with wary eyes.

"What did you think of them?" Carmen asked.

Think of the cyborg whom she'd spoken with, other than the fact that he was big, sexy, and kissed better than any of her ex-boyfriends? "That they're definitely not the bloodthirsty killers the military wants us to believe."

"I'd have to agree. They are not what I expected," Carmen said, tossing her hair over her shoulder with a coy look upward.

"Why, because they haven't murdered us yet or ch-chopped us up for parts?" Percy and his negative attitude. Why was he so determined to believe the worst?

Riley coughed so she wouldn't laugh. "Um, I think those parts in the news have been grossly exaggerated."

"D-d-did you not see the c-c-carnage when they took over the installation?"

"Yes. And I also saw what so-called humans did to the other prisoners, as well as some of us present." She swept a hand at the mute women who sat huddled in their corner. "If you ask me, we're better off now. At least the cyborgs rely on logic."

"How does that help?"

"Because as long as their logic dictates they can use us, they won't harm us." *I think.* Because meant as a punishment or not, she didn't count the kiss as a deterrent.

"And they're men. Men without any women on board." Again, Carmen played to the camera, posing and licking her full lips.

Riley wanted to roll her eyes. *Could she be any more obvious?*

"You'd sleep with them?" Percy wrinkled his nose.

"Screw, not sleep. Cyborgs like to fuck as much as any other man." Carmen's bluntness made Riley's cheeks heat.

"And you know this because?"

"It doesn't take a genius to spot a hard-on. Where there's an erection, there's a chance for seduction."

Riley's elation in the kiss evaporated. Had her cyborg captor embraced Carmen too? Did he do it to all the female prisoners? She didn't dare ask. She feared appearing stupid in front of the others, especially since she'd thought it something spur of the moment on his part. *Stupid me thinking we'd shared something.* It would wound her pride if she found out she wasn't the only one.

"So what do we d-d-do now?" Percy asked.

"We wait." Wait to see if the cyborgs would let them live, or, if as Percy feared, they'd die. In Riley's case, she also wondered if the big guy would attempt another kiss, or more.

Chapter Ten

Aramus sent the little female packing, but she wouldn't leave his thoughts. As he strode down his ship's halls to the sickbay, he couldn't help but recall their conversation—and kiss.

What a puzzle Riley proved to be, one moment boldly questioning him, the next cowering as if fearful of retaliation. It made him want to kill the people running the place all over again, this time in a more painful manner, which in turn made him question if he was functioning at one hundred percent capacity.

Why do I fucking care? Why does her treatment at their hands make me so bloody angry? Analysis deduced that his rage seemed to stem from pity, pity for a human. What the fuck was that about? Retaliation because of the harm done to Avion and the other cyborgs he could understand. They shared a bond. They were a sort of family. But she was nothing. Nothing but a prisoner who had information he needed. *And I need another kiss.* Where had that stray thought come from? Surely not him.

Argh! So unacceptable. Perhaps he'd not worked off enough energy during the fight. Or his adrenaline still ran high. Once he'd spoken to Avion, he was heading straight for the gym. Hit some weights. Punch a few bags. Sweat up a storm. Perhaps then he could convince his body to behave in a proper manner. *I am in control, and you will obey.* Easy enough to say now with Riley gone from his presence, but he couldn't help but wonder if the malfunction would reoccur if he were to spend time in her presence again. His curious side urged him to test it. His logical one screamed danger. A lobotomy to remove his feelings was looking more and more attractive all the time.

Arriving at the medical bay, he entered to find Avion reclining in a seated position and looking better. More accurately, cleaner. While they'd washed and bathed the cyborg, giving his hair and jaw a much-needed trim, he still appeared as frail as before, his injuries still glaringly evident.

MJ, the only cyborg with some medical training on board, fiddled with dusty IV tubes, attempting to insert them in Avion's wrists, which bore the marks of already having been overused as a pincushion.

"What the fuck are you doing?"

"Trying to get some fluids in him."

"So dump some down his throat."

MJ shot him a glare. "Gee. Thanks for the suggestion. Never thought of it."

"Don't get mad at him," Avion rasped. "I've tried drinking, but my stomach is rebelling. It's been so long since I've eaten anything that my body is rejecting it."

"I'm attempting to rehydrate him via more traditional medical methods since skin absorption by his nanos also failed."

The news shocked Aramus. He'd never heard of any cyborg nanos failing before. Coursing through their bloodstream, and permeating every part of their body, the nanobots were like mini computers regulating and fixing their bodies. It was part of what made them cyborg and made them strong. Without them...they were no better than a human. "Have you attempted a reboot to get his nanos functioning?"

"Rebooting did not help. I attempted a connection to our onboard medical diagnostic computer and a few other things. His body keeps rejecting all attempts to get his nanos functioning."

"What did they do to you?" Aramus spoke his inner musing aloud.

"It would take less time to list the things they didn't," Avion replied, a wan smile twisting his lips.

"Why don't we start with how the fuck you survived. I thought you blew up with that ship back when we raided that asteroid."

"I did, but I got lucky, or not I guess, depending on how you look at it. I ended up protected from the worst of the blast by the shield around the command center, but I was heavily damaged so my BCI shut me down while my nanos repaired me. A salvage unit picked me up. I woke to find myself in an electrified cage surrounded by lead with no way in or out, not even to send a message."

"Military?"

"That's what I suspected initially until I realized the soldiers spoke all kinds of languages and wore civilian uniforms, not federation ones."

"So you've been their prisoner all this time?" Not good. Given his depleted state, Aramus wondered how many cyborg secrets Avion had revealed, intentionally or not.

Something of his worries must have shown on his face because Avion spoke as if he'd read his mind. "Yes, I've been a captive, but don't worry about our secrets. I guarded those well. I shut down my pain receptors as soon as I realized I was a POW. I also wiped my memory banks of all items pertaining to the cyborg escape."

"Our home planet location is safe?"

"So safe I couldn't have found it even if I did escape, which they let me do once when they realized torture wasn't getting them anywhere."

"I don't recall hearing about any attempts of you contacting us."

"Because I couldn't. I wiped everything to keep you safe. The only things I retained were the knowledge of our liberation, who I was, and what I went through. I used those as my focal points when things got rough. Everything else is gone. I didn't wander for long before they picked me back up to resume their testing."

"Did you keep a detailed log of your treatment at their hands?"

"I did."

MJ, done with his tubes and fiddling, interrupted. "We downloaded it when we attempted to re-boot his nanos. We're hoping Einstein or someone can go through the memories and figure out how to reverse the damage done to his cyborg systems. I've never seen anything like it. It's as if his machine parts are there, but his body is using them as they would the fleshy human version. It's why he's healing so slowly. For all intents and purposes, despite his upgrades, Avion is human."

Aramus reeled from the shocking conclusion, horrified. He couldn't imagine a life without his upgrades. Much as he hated what had been done to him, he could admit he was an improved version of his former human self. To go from strong to weak? It appalled him to the extreme.

He squeezed Avion's shoulder, glad the currently blind cyborg couldn't see his pity. Avion discerned it anyhow.

"Don't feel sorry for me. I am cyborg. I can be repaired. I will emerge stronger than ever. And when I do…"

"We'll kill those responsible, together."

After his visit with Avion, he checked on the new cyborg additions. The female remained sedated as her body healed itself, her nanos responding properly. The other male cyborg they'd picked up had been debriefed but couldn't provide much information. It seemed he'd spent years on an outpost, on his own, and had only recently arrived at the hidden installation.

He seemed pleased at his change in circumstances, especially the knowledge that cyborgs no longer took orders from humans. It didn't mean Aramus granted him any quarter. Until the new units went through a complete debriefing and debugging, none of them would have unrestricted access to the ship or their computers. Who knew what hidden time bombs possibly hid within their bodies? It wouldn't be the first time the military or company turned a cyborg into a walking weapon.

Aphelion contacted Aramus to let him know he'd gotten all he could glean from the installation's computers.

"At this point, there's nothing left for me to copy."

"Good. I don't like staying here. We're too easy a target. Prepare the ship for takeoff."

"Aye, sir."

"Oh, and Aphelion."

"Yes."

"Let me know when we've reached a safe distance for the deployment of a nuke."

Because no way was Aramus leaving this place of torture intact. As he stared a while later at the smoking ruins of the mountain and the horrors he'd found inside, he couldn't help his grim, *One down, but how many more to go?*

Followed by, *And where the fuck is Seth?*

Chapter Eleven

A day went by. Locked in their large cell, the prisoners found themselves bored, talk having petered out as they each sat on their pallets, mulling their situation. The comatose guy was taken away on the pretext of caring for him. The mute women, who kept to themselves, huddled in a corner, eyeing Percy with suspicion and rejecting any overtures Riley and Carmen made.

With nothing to entertain them, silence reigned, and Riley took that time to let her imagination run rampant as she wondered what to expect next. She'd not seen the big cyborg since his questioning the day before, just their guard, who slid food packets into their cell and stubbornly refused to answer any of their questions.

While Carmen played to the camera, Riley refused to look at it even as a part of her wondered if *he* watched. If he did, then he got an eyeful of cleavage as Carmen had unzipped her jumpsuit far enough to leave little to the imagination, claiming she was too warm. Funny, because Riley personally found their space chilly and would have assumed Carmen did too given how she was showing headlights in the upper chest area.

Uncharitable or not, she couldn't help but label the psychologist as a hussy. Here they were, waiting to see if freedom, death, or some third unknown option awaited them, and all Carmen could seem to think about was seducing their captors. The fact that Riley relived her one kiss over and over didn't seem hypocritical, in her mind at least. Yes, she'd enjoyed the embrace, but that didn't mean she flaunted her assets and practically masturbated for an unseen audience.

When the summons came, one by one they were led from the room, but didn't return. First the mute women, then Percy. Carmen left with a bright smile for their guard and a, "Hey, handsome", until only Riley was left, a very nervous Riley who wondered if their time was up.

Is this where it ends? After all she'd been through, had she gotten saved only to end up dead because of the ongoing ill treatment by the same people who screwed up her life in the first place? The irony of it wasn't lost on her.

When her time came, she struggled to remain brave, holding her spine straight as she found herself marched to a different area of the ship by the same non-communicative cyborg as before.

"Where are we going?" To her surprise he answered, yet didn't.

"This way."

"What's this way?

"Our destination."

"Why?"

"Because Aramus said so."

How she wanted to scream and yank on his hair for his useless answers. "Who is Aramus?"

Growled from behind was an "I am." Riley whirled to see the big bald guy who'd questioned—and kissed her—sneak up on them. "Any more questions?"

"Actually, yes."

"Why am I not surprised?" he muttered. "You can go now, Smith. I've got her." Wrapping his fingers around her upper arm, he practically dragged her down the hall.

"Your name is Aramus?"

"I thought I'd already confirmed that."

"Are you the leader of this ship?"

"Who leads is not knowledge you require, unless you're a spy." He halted all of a sudden, and she stumbled. Only his grip on her arm kept her upright. It also meant when she flailed, his body was what her hands found to steady her. He wore a T-shirt that hugged his massive upper body so when her hands splayed out across his chest, the heat of him seeped through the thin fabric, surprising her. She'd not noticed it before during their embrace.

She couldn't help but say, "You're so warm."

"As opposed to what. Cold?"

She flushed. "Last time we spoke I hadn't noted it." She lied. She'd thought the extreme heat of his touch a result of her own feverish reply to his embrace.

"Cyborgs tend to run a few degrees hotter than humans, although we can drop that if required."

"Why would you need to make yourself colder?"

"Most detection units search for heat signatures. When planning an ambush or invasion, masking this allows for a smoother infiltration."

That made sense. "I'm surprised you're telling me this. Didn't you just accuse me of being a spy?"

He shrugged. "Our ability to regulate our core temperature is common knowledge."

"What else is common knowledge about your kind?" Only once it left her lips did she realize how it sounded. As if she saw him as something else, someone who wasn't like her. *Then again, I'd say it's pretty obvious he isn't like me.* Human perhaps a long time ago, he'd made it clear he no longer thought of himself as on the same level as her.

His lips curled in derision. "My *kind*," he said, stressing the word, "are stronger, faster, and smarter. We are hotter than the average human. The males are bigger, both height and body mass wise. We are also dexterous, logical when it comes to acting and unforgiving when it comes to dealing with enemies, or spies." He fixed his glare on her, in an attempt to intimidate.

For some reason, it didn't make her cringe. "Oh, for god's sake. I am not a spy. Exactly who would I report to? And how? Not to mention why? Those jerks treated me like crap. I wouldn't call nine-one-one if they were on fire."

"But if the choice came down to saving a human or cyborg, we both know which you'd chose."

"The one who deserved it most."

"Then I guess I would be screwed," drawled Aramus with mocking sarcasm.

"Don't be so sure of that. You might act Mr. Big and Tough, but I'll bet you're just a big old softy inside." Why she said it she couldn't have said, but she couldn't help but laugh as his eyebrows shot up in comical fashion at her claim.

"I am not soft."

"Sure you aren't."

"Hit me, you'll see."

"I didn't mean physically. I meant, I'll bet you care more than you think and not just about cyborgs."

"Caring is not in my programming."

"And I say bull. You can't hide the fact you feel things."

"Emotions are for the weak."

"That's where you're wrong. Emotions are what make us stronger. It's what makes us fight when the easier thing to do would be to give up. If you ask me, cyborgs care a lot. Why else would you hate humans for what they've done and seek vengeance?"

"We seek vengeance so we can have peace."

"If you wanted peace, you'd leave and never return. Yet you want something from humanity. Revenge, answers, acceptance. Which is it?"

"None," he snapped. "But if you don't stop pestering me, I will kill you."

"No you won't."

Again, he rumbled. "Why do you persist in thinking me incapable of meting violence? I could snap your neck this instant and feel no remorse."

"Says the guy who's been real careful not to hurt me." She eyed her arm, which, while held by him, was in no danger of bruising.

"You are really pissing me off."

"I know, and yet you still haven't slapped me around, killed me, or turned me into a mute, just reinforcing my belief. You're a big marshmallow inside." As his brows drew together to form one dark line, and the steam practically burst from his ears, she couldn't help but giggle, even as she wondered at her own sanity. *Do I have a death wish? Why the hell am I bugging him this way?*

"Take that back."

"No." Why she taunted the scary cyborg she couldn't say, yet tease him she did, certainty her shield. *I hope I am right because, otherwise, I've gone insane and am about to die.*

"You are supposed to fear me," he bellowed, tightening his clamp, but still not injuring her. Had he wanted to, he could have crushed her arm to a pulp. Slammed her against a wall. Done any number of things that would have shut her up. Her human employers had required much less reason than this to inflict pain.

"I would if I thought you'd actually hurt me. But you won't. And you don't scare me." She stood her ground and met his annoyed glare with a steady one. For anyone monitoring her heart rate at the moment, it would have seemed she lied, as it raced faster than normal. But she was a doctor, and she knew the true cause. Attraction. The more he denied the empathy and gentleness within him, the more she found him attractive. The more she wanted a repeat of their kiss. The more…

A head poked out of a room up the hall. "If you're done yelling at the female, mind bringing her in? Avion is quite curious to meet the human with a death wish."

"Who's Avion?" she asked as she found herself dragged behind Aramus.

"One of the cyborgs you claim to have not seen while working at the installation."

That was the only warning she got before he yanked her into a room and she came face to face with the cyborg he called Avion. *Oh that poor man.*

Moisture brimmed on her lashes, and she bit her lip lest she gasp. Before, when she'd examined the tortured bodies of the experiments brought to her, she'd found it easy to keep a professional distance. She'd never met or spoken to them. Never known them when they lived.

However, the poor man before her? He bore the marks of abuse, the face of someone haunted, and was living proof of the evil that she'd worked under. It didn't take a doctor, or even a genius, to see he was a shell of the man he used to be. One only had to see the skin that hung loosely on his frame to guess he'd lost a lot of weight, most of it muscle. Scars and bruises crisscrossed his exposed upper chest and arms, further proof of the mistreatment he'd suffered at human hands. A bandage covered his eyes, but she could guess what lay beneath. She'd seen it before on her table, orbs missing as the scientists kept them for who knew what reason. All of these things combined, tore at her, made her cry for this cyborg she'd never met but instantly felt empathy for.

"Oh, you poor thing," she murmured. "What did they do to you?"

"As I keep saying, it would be easier to ask what they didn't," quipped the cyborg with wry humor.

"How can you joke about it?"

"Because I can't cry. Besides, what would lamenting accomplish? I am cyborg. I will heal. Eventually. I hope."

"What do you mean?"

"Nothing," barked Aramus. "I take it you're going to claim like your friends that you've never met him before?"

"No. Like I said, I dealt with bodies, not the living. And I never had a cyborg end up on my table."

"Are you sure?"

Turning to glance at Aramus, she found him studying her instead of the cyborg on the bed. "Yes, I'm sure. Or would you like to accuse me of lying again?"

"Isn't that what humans do best?"

"Not all of us."

He made a sound similar to the one her grandfather made when no one would agree with his views on the political mess in the world.

She sighed. "Believe it or not, I am not your enemy. I also don't understand why you've brought me here. What exactly do you want from me?"

"Can you tell me what they did?"

"How would I know? I told you, I never saw him before."

"But you're more than passing familiar with the results of what they did. I want you to examine

Avion and see if he bears some of the testing you remarked on the corpses you autopsied."

"You can't be serious."

"Why the fuck not?"

"Well, for one thing, because he's alive."

"And?"

"I deal with dead things."

"There're not much different. They all have the same parts, more or less."

"There's a lot different. For one, corpses don't bleed or scream if I need to cut them open."

"Hold on, Doctor, no one said anything about cutting," Avion interjected.

"And I don't intend to. I'd say you've been through enough already." She crossed her arms and glared at Aramus, daring him to contradict, once again testing his patience. If he didn't like it, then too freaking bad. He could threaten all he wanted, even make her suffer, but she would not become one of the monsters she hated.

"Would you both not jump to illogical conclusions? When I said examine, I meant in general. Visually."

"Oh." She flushed at her misconception, and Avion chuckled as he said, "Well, that's a relief."

"You're both idiots," Aramus muttered.

"I'll need some gloves."

"What for? Are you planning to stick a digit somewhere and make me cough?"

Riley didn't know who looked more startled at Avion's jest, her or Aramus. "First off, I am not sticking my finger in any holes, most especially not that one. And second, the gloves are for sanitary reasons. I always use them so I don't catch anything."

"Cyborgs are impervious to disease," Aramus announced.

Avion took her side. "She should wear the gloves."

Riley sensed an undercurrent to their words and wondered at the quiet, which stretched as Aramus frowned at the injured cyborg. After a few moments, he nodded, saying, "You're right."

Huh? Did I miss something? Riley definitely felt like something had been said between the men, but if that was the case, they'd done so telepathically, which, given they were cyborgs, was entirely possible. Whatever the case, they scrounged up a dusty box of gloves at the back of a cabinet, and she snapped them on before approaching Avion.

"Good news, you don't have any extra limbs," she announced as she set her hands on his ribcage and began palpating him.

"Or a tail," Avion joked. "Did you see a lot of deformities in the bodies you examined?"

"Yes and no. A lot of the changes weren't readily evident. It was only when I cut them open that I really noted the differences, although, in most cases, the skin color gave it away. Without fail, the corpses were varying shades of gray."

"But they were human?"

"As I told your boss," she said, ignoring Aramus, who loomed over her shoulder watching her every move, "it is my belief they were mixing foreign DNA with human, trying to make something new."

"Did they ever succeed?"

She shrugged. "I never saw any living gray people if that's what you're asking."

"How did they die?"

"Violently and intentionally. Bullets to the head being the most common cause of death."

"The second most common method?"

"Decapitation."

"Are you fucking kidding me?" Aramus seemed shocked.

"I wish. The headless corpses were also, without fail, the ones who least resembled humans. They were the ones with tails, and extra arms. Some even sported spiny ridges. It was disturbing to say the least. They looked almost like devils."

"Did they have horns?" Aramus mocked.

"No idea. I never saw the heads in those instances."

"What do you think they did with them?"

She shrugged as she moved lower from Avion's ribs to palpate his stomach, her fingers sinking into the sunken cavity, so unlike the hard abdomen of the cyborg breathing down her neck. "Your guess is as good as mine. Maybe they pickled them and put them on a shelf as part of a collection."

"Damn. I wish our searching team had found one."

She shuddered. "Why?"

"Our scientists would have wanted to examine them."

"Scientists? I thought all cyborgs were soldiers."

"Most, but not all," Avion replied. "Our kind is—"

"She doesn't need a lesson in cyborg divisions," Aramus interrupted. "And what do you think you're doing?"

"Examining Avion as you ordered." In the process of probing his hips with her fingertips, Riley did her best to keep her gaze averted from his groin area.

"Would you like some privacy while you fondle him?" Aramus snapped.

She stopped and whirled to face him. "What is your problem? I'm doing what you asked me to do." And yet, he seemed irrationally angry. She just couldn't understand why. *If I didn't know better, I'd say he was jealous.*

Chapter Twelve

Aramus didn't know where the rage came from. It bore no rational basis. Riley did as told. She examined Avion, her manner professional, her bedside manner gentle and courteous. But as soon as she pulled that sheet down and exposed Avion's lower regions, more specifically his cock, which reacted to her clinical touch, Aramus found himself suddenly imbued with anger—and an urge to punch his friend before throwing her over his shoulder and carrying her away.

What is wrong with me? To his surprise, his BCI had a ready reply. Jealousy.

What the fuck? No way. Aramus did not care that the doctor touched Avion. She did her job. Reminding himself didn't stem the anger—or halt the urge to kiss her when she faced him with flashing eyes and pursed lips.

He tried to justify his actions. "I am just ensuring that you are not taking advantage of Avion. He is blind and cannot see what you are doing."

"Actually, she can take advantage of me all she wants," Avion interjected. "Do you know how long it's been since a woman touched me down there?" He smiled.

Aramus clenched his fist at his side lest he rip the grin from Avion's face. "This is a medical examination, not a date or foreplay. I expect you both to comport yourselves in a professional manner."

"I am," she stated, eyes still flashing in irritation. "It's you who's acting all crazy. If you can't handle watching, then maybe you should step into the hall and wait until I'm done."

"You'd like that, wouldn't you? Leave you alone with our medical equipment so you can tamper with it. Give you a chance to plant one of your human programming bombs in my friend's mind or kill him so he can't tell us what he knows."

Her mouth rounded into an O of astonishment. "You're nuts. Completely and utterly whacked."

"There is nothing wrong with my cognitive abilities."

"Ha. I think you should check again."

They both turned as Avion chuckled. "You two are funny."

"I see nothing amusing about the situation."

"Ditto," replied Riley.

"Oh please. Aramus, you and I both know the human won't harm me and that there's nothing she can use or do here that would cause harm. Not with the cameras watching. And she's right. You are acting in a most irrational manner. I understand your concern for my well-being, but rest assured, even without my sight, it would take more than this female to kill me. No offense, Doctor."

"None taken, and thank you."

Having his momentary lapse of reasoning so soundly spanked, made Aramus clamp his lips into a tight line and take a step back. He said not a word as Riley completed her examination, her hands not once touching Avion's male parts—thank fuck, because Aramus wasn't quite sure what he would have done.

At the completion of her visual exam, she peeled off the gloves with a rubberized snap and disposed of them. "He's normal."

"Normal as in?"

She shrugged. "Honestly? Normal for a human. If I didn't know he was cyborg, I would never have known. He shows no physical signs of being anything other than what he is. An undernourished male in his late twenties, with outward signs of physical abuse. His skeletal structure is what I'd expect. His skin pallor is not even close to gray. And while I didn't see his organs, he shows no misshapen lumps or bulges indicating oversized or extra ones. If he were a regular patient, I'd say he needs rest, food, and exercise. But that's mostly just common sense. Again, I'm not an expert on living things."

Aramus pulled up the sheet over Avion, higher than before. "So he was not subjected to the DNA experimentation?"

"Not according to my visual exam. But you'll want to run a blood test and take tissue samples to be sure."

Already done. The stuttering idiot Percy was running the diagnostic in another room under Kentry's watchful eyes. The comatose human would have been the better choice to do it given his qualifications, but since he'd yet to wake, they made do with the resources they had.

"We shall leave you to rest, Avion."

"So soon? And here I was hoping to chitchat with the doctor for a bit?" Blind or not, Avion had no problem directing a grin Riley's way.

Friends do not punch friends for smiling at humans. Aramus ran this message in a loop as he once again clamped his hand around Riley's upper arm and guided her from the room with a gruff, "I'll be back later to check on you."

"Bye," Riley called out before the door slid shut. "Well, that was rude of you," she remarked as he marched her up the hall.

"What was?"

"The way you hustled us out of there like the room was on fire."

"We were done."

"I know we were done, but would it have killed you to say a proper goodbye? Or to offer your friend some reassurance or congrats on passing the physical?"

"Avion is not a child who needs his hand held. He understood the results and does not require pointless chatter about my leave-taking."

"I don't disagree with anything you said. But you missed the real point. It's called manners. You know, that thing known as common courtesy that you should extend to everyone, especially friends who are probably a little wigged out still from their experience."

Aramus couldn't help but sneer. "Manners? We are cyborg. What need do we have of those?"

"None. Yet considering how high and mighty you deem yourself, would it hurt you to show some?"

"You are aggravating."

"Yet polite, even when you're acting like an ass." She smiled at him. He growled. She smiled wider.

"Please and thank you are a waste of time and oxygen."

"So is pointless arguing, yet you seem to have no trouble with that."

"Don't force me to shut you up." With the erection he couldn't seem to tame. Why did his ridiculous argument with the female have him harder than a steel girder? He had no problem tuning out the other annoying female he'd picked up. His dick behaved even though she kept blatantly displaying her feminine attributes. Yet this tiny doctor, with her goading remarks, smiles, and lack of fear, even when he barked, roused him. Enflamed him, messed with his circuits, and all without a single touch. No one had ever managed that before.

"Hmm, do you intend to shut me up like you did last time?"

She seemed just as surprised as he did by her reference to the kiss, but once out there, Aramus couldn't help but remember it. The way her lips felt under his. How her body fit. It seemed he wasn't alone in recalling that erotic moment. His sensors picked up the change in her body; her pulse raced, and her womanly musk, signaling arousal, enveloped him.

Not in control of his own limbs, he found himself bracketing her body in the hall, one hand flat on the wall on either side of her head. He leaned down until they were nose to nose. He stared into her wide blue eyes. Her breath caught. He waited for her to beg him to move away, for fear to take over and cloud her gaze. Instead…she rubbed the tip of his nose with hers.

"What are you doing?"

"Eskimo kiss."

Seriously? Laughter barked from him, unexpected and loud. "I can't believe you just did that."

An impish smile tilted her lips, and her eyes sparkled. "Me either. But you looked like you needed it."

"No. What I need," *want*, "is this." He pressed his mouth to hers. Big mistake. Most awesome malfunction ever.

The two theories clashed, but he ignored the logical part of his BCI warning him he should move away in favor of experiencing what only Riley seemed to evoke: passion. True passion. The kind that made his blood boil, his electronic heart race, and his mind sink into chaos.

Defective action on his part, but the pleasure, oh, the pleasure of her soft lips against his, her panting breath, and the way she clutched at him made him welcome the aberration.

Until he heard the stomp of approaching feet. He couldn't tear himself away fast enough. Just in time too as Xylo rounded the corner.

"Everything all right, sir?" Xylo asked with his head tilted at an angle.

"Fine. Just taking our prisoner to her new quarters."

"Would you like me to do that for you? I was heading in that direction."

First impulse? No. He'd take her himself. Her quarters had privacy and a bed. Wrong answer. "If you could. I have more important matters to attend to."

He ignored the unmistakable flash of hurt that flitted across her face and told himself he didn't care.

She didn't remain injured for long, not judging by the way she snapped, "Is it time to chug a gallon of crude oil to lube your mechanical joints?"

"Now who's being rude?" he taunted. Why the flash of not one but two of her middle fingers made him smile he couldn't have said, nor could he resist a parting, "Bye, bye, Doctor. Have a pleasant evening."

No manners. Ha. He'd just shown her.

Chapter Thirteen

Insufferable jerk, mocking her at every turn while at the same time sending out mixed signals. One moment he kissed her as if he couldn't get enough, and the next he jumped away from her as if she bore the plague—to which he was immune.

He's afraid of my human cooties. That or he was embarrassed and fearful one of his buddies might catch him kissing a human. *Well, maybe I don't want to be caught kissing a machine.* The petty thought instantly sobered her. No matter what she'd been taught, or what Aramus did or said to convince her, she couldn't equate the man she'd left behind with an unemotional robot. His kiss was too hot and too real to deny. Metallic parts, computer things in his brain or not, Aramus was nothing like a machine. Nothing like anyone she'd ever met.

Oh god, don't tell me I'm suffering from that syndrome where a prisoner falls for her captor. A valid theory, except she'd never wanted to drag any of her human abusers in for a smooch, and more…

Eyeing the ramrod back of the cyborg in front of her, she debated questioning him. Unlike her previous guard, this one exuded an aura of don't-mess-with-me, and she wasn't entirely confident he'd restrain himself as well as Aramus and the others did. But it didn't stop her.

"I'm Riley."

"I know."

It seemed a lack of manners was the norm among the cyborg. "And you are?"

"Xylo." Curt, but at least he replied.

Interesting name. "Nice to meet you, Xylo." He grunted. Not the communicative type, but so far not the violent kind either. She forged ahead. "Do you know what's in store for us?"

"No."

She ventured another query. "I heard Aramus say we're going to some new quarters. Will the others be there too?"

"No."

"Are they dead?"

"No."

"Where are they?"

He shrugged without turning or replying.

She ground her back teeth. "Anyone ever tell you that you suck at chitchat?"

Uh-oh. His head rotated in that freaky way cyborgs had, especially given he continued to walk in an unerring line without hitting a wall. The coldness in his gaze sent a shiver down her spine.

"I am not here for your entertainment nor to answer your numerous questions. For the moment, you are, against my advice, passengers on our ship and as such will be accorded a modicum of liberty. Step out of line, or show yourself to be a nuisance, and rest assured, what little freedom we are granting will be terminated. Do I make myself clear?"

Nodding, she swallowed any other questions she had. Where she trusted Aramus to restrain himself, she had her doubts about this guy. He seemed to want an excuse. *Well, I'm not giving him one.* He halted a moment later in front a door.

"These are your new quarters. You will be monitored at all times while within them and when you leave."

"You're not locking me in?"

"No. But, again, that is contingent on your behavior. Computer access has been disabled for you and your companions, so do not attempt to hack your way into our system. Such an act will be dealt with in a harsh manner."

"I suck with computers, so no worries there, but what if I need to talk to someone?" Like Aramus.

"Use the command, 'computer I wish to speak to' and the name of the person you seek. A communication channel will be opened, but keep in mind, all conversations will be monitored."

"Yup. I get it. No privacy. Does this extend to when I pee? Going to listen to that too?" Tired of his attitude, which reeked of distrust, she couldn't help the sarcasm.

He didn't deign to reply but continued his speech. "The mess hall is down this corridor, fifth door to your left. The common room is across from it. You may use both. The command center and engine rooms are off limits, as are crew quarters unless by invitation."

"What about the medical bay?"

"What need do you have of the medical area?"

"I met Avion today and thought perhaps he'd like some company. Unlike others around here, he seems to have a sense of humor."

"One moment while I ask." His eyes lost focus for a moment, and this time there was no mistaking it. He was talking to someone. He replied a moment later. "Aramus says you may, but you are not to perform any procedures on Avion or anyone else."

"Darn, no game of Operation? And here I was wondering if Avion would beep if the tweezers touched the side." The joke went right over his head, as expected, so it didn't surprise her when with one final derisive sneer, Xylo pivoted on his heel and left.

Alone, Riley took stock of her new room. Small, it made her think of her dorm days with its single bed tightly made with a gray woolen blanket and flat pillow. Above the bed was a dusty shelf, empty of knickknacks. Along the wall across from the foot of the bed were two sliding doors. One opened onto a barren closet, the other, a tiny washroom with a basic toilet, sink and, oh yes, a shower. She couldn't strip fast enough once she saw it.

Under the hot spray, she groaned. Heaven. It was only as she lathered up with the liquid soap that squirted from the built-in dispenser that she recalled Xylo's warning they would watch and listen at all times.

Suddenly aware, she peeked up, trying to see if she could spot the camera, or had the cyborg lied? It didn't really matter in the end. She needed to finish washing, so pretending she was alone, she soaped and rinsed, and if her hands rubbed longer, and more sensually than usual, she blamed the pleasure of the hot water on her actions.

Chapter Fourteen

Alone in his quarters, Aramus clenched his fists as he spied on Riley. *I am no better than a scummy human.* A perverted one, who watched as a woman bathed. Knowing what he did was wrong, that he was acting like a voyeur, didn't stop him. He could no more shut off the live feed than he could close his eyes. The one thing he did do, though, was block any others from watching.

What that said about him, he preferred not to think of. The fact he'd not blocked any of the cameras in the other prisoner rooms didn't sway his decision. The fact he'd not bothered checking in on any of the other humans didn't stop him or have him questioning his actions. The fact his hand cupped his aching cock and squeezed it only made him stare more ardently at the unfolding scene.

So innocent. Just a woman washing herself, and yet, he'd never seen anything so sensually decadent. The water gave Riley's skin a shiny sheen. The water rolled down the plentiful curves of her body, their roundness so temptingly different than his previous experiences. How he envied her hands as they stroked across her slick flesh. How he longed to lap at the droplets of moisture that dripped from the tips of her nipples. What he wouldn't give to slide his hand…

With a harsh cry, he came, his cock jerking in his grip, and yet, he didn't feel sated. As a matter of fact, his ardor seemed worse than before.

Forcing his eyes shut, he turned from the screen and breathed deep, even if he didn't require the oxygen, in and out. He needed to do something to quell his tumultuous heart.

What is wrong with me?

Why did he stalk this female? Why could he not put her from his mind? Why did she cause him to lose control over his own body—and mind?

With a growl, he stood and entered his washroom, quickly rinsing the evidence of his shame and changing into a clean pair of pants. He then summoned MJ.

The cyborg arrived at Aramus's quarters, and the door had barely shut before Aramus said, "I need you to reset me."

"Excuse me?"

"My BCI. I need a full reboot."

"Why don't you do it yourself?"

"I have. But I must not be doing it right because I'm still not functioning correctly."

"You're going to have to explain better."

Explain? Explain how he lusted after a human female and have MJ mock him and know his shame? "I'd rather jam a screwdriver in my ear and see if it works."

MJ snorted, thinking he jested, but his expression soon turned more serious. "Holy shit. You mean that?"

"Yes. Something is wrong with me, and I think it's affecting my judgment."

"Do you need to relinquish control of the ship?"

"No. That part of my mind is functioning correctly. It's another part that's not." He gave a pointed look down.

MJ appeared confused for a moment then understanding dawned. "Ah, having a penile problem. It happens."

"I am not impotent." Aramus couldn't clarify fast enough.

"Then what's wrong with your cock? Burning sensation? Unusual growth? Leakage?"

"Try unwanted erection."

MJ snickered. "So?"

"So, it's pissing me off. It won't go away."

Laughter boomed from the onboard doctor. "It's not that big of a deal. You're horny. Happens to all of us and it's easy to fix. No need to fetch a screwdriver and go to extremes, just masturbate."

"I've tried that. Numerous times, but my cock refuses to stand down."

"What's triggering it? Wait, I'll bet I know what, or should I say who? One of the females we picked up. Is it the cyborg female?"

Aramus shuddered. While he'd not spoken to her yet, he'd seen her file and image. "Fuck no. The only thing differentiating her from a man is her tits. No, it's not the cyborg female. It's a…human." Saying it aloud brought an odd heat to his cheeks, an uncontrollable change in temperature. *Oh for fucks sake, don't tell me I'm goddamn blushing.* Could his sickness get any worse?

"Which one?"

Wasn't it obvious? "The attractive one."

"Carmen?"

Aramus frowned. "No. I meant the doctor. Riley."

"Oh. The chubby one." MJ disparaged her, and Aramus almost punched him out. Yes, the doctor had a curvy physique, but Aramus found the curves suited her, gave her a sensual appeal. MJ shrugged. "So you find her cute. I don't see the problem."

Was MJ truly that dense? Aramus spelled it out for him. "The problem is I desire her."

"Easy solution then; screw her."

"Screw her? That's your remedy? Screw her?"

"Well, you said masturbating didn't work."

"It didn't."

"So, do what your body wants and get back to normal. Have sex."

"But I don't want to have sex with her." He was such a liar.

"But you just said—"

"I know what I fucking said. However, I don't want to. I hate humans."

"Not that one."

"All of them."

MJ rolled his eyes in a manner not befitting a proper cyborg. "Oh, would you stop fucking arguing? You like her. You want to bang her. So do it. Do it twice. Three times. This will clear your system without the need for a lobotomy or a screwdriver."

"There's no other way?" Aramus tamped down his body's excited response as he asked in a morose tone.

"No. As your chief medical officer, I command you to obey. Fuck the human."

Well, when he put it that way, how could he disobey? It seemed a little extreme as a medical treatment, but it wouldn't be the first time Aramus had sacrificed himself, this time for his own good instead of for others.

Chapter Fifteen

A day went by. One long, freaking day of boredom as Riley paced her room, and when she got tired of those four walls, she walked the hall. At mealtime, she ate cardboard rations. She tried to sit and watch a movie with the other prisoners, but the only videos on board were documentaries. She even visited Avion, but he slept, so she left and returned to the lounge area where she attempted to engage the others in conversation. Percy proved too hard to converse with, and the mute women had disappeared, apparently refusing to leave the safety of the room they shared. Carmen left claiming she had a date, and David was still in a coma.

Of cyborgs, she saw none, not even Aramus, who had made himself scarce, in person at least, but she had the sensation he kept tabs on her. She couldn't have exactly explained why, other than a vague sense of being watched. It prickled at her skin, made her jumpy, and left her vaguely disappointed when, at the end of her first full day of freedom, she'd not run into him.

It occurred to her the next day, after a night spent dreaming of the big cyborg—him wearing nothing but trousers while doing pushups as she straddled his back counting—that she could ask to speak to him. Perhaps claim she'd remembered something important, but that smacked too much of desperation, especially considering the only thing of import she could think to tell him was that the food sucked.

So she languished, rousing only a little when the engines stirred to life, signaling a change in speed and departure from the galaxy that had held her prisoner. About time. Wondering if the others had any news, she headed to the common room.

"We're leaving this galaxy?" she asked, entering to find Carmen filing her nails.

"Yes. They didn't find any signs of pursuit, so we're off."

Riley didn't question Carmen's sources. She was too afraid she'd find out Aramus had told her—while naked in bed. "Where are we heading?"

"Their home planet once they make sure we're not being followed and that none of us are harboring tracking devices."

"Their what? You mean we're not going home to earth?"

Carmen paused in her manicure long enough to shoot her a look of disdain. "No, not earth. Don't tell me you were foolish enough to ever think that would happen."

Actually, she was. "But what about our families? And friends? We need to tell them we're safe."

A snort blew past Carmen's full lips. "Holy shit. Are you truly that stupid?"

Bristling at the insult, Riley pursed her lips as she replied, "What do you mean?"

"You're dead."

Riley looked down at herself then back at Carmen. "Um, I hate to point out the obvious, but, no, I'm not."

"You are to everyone back on earth. Or did you really think the company that took us would leave any loose ends? All of us, me, Percy, David, those women, yourself, all of us had tragic accidents back on earth, not long after we came to work for them."

"What are you talking about?"

"You poor naïve thing. I thought you knew. In order to ensure our families wouldn't look into our disappearance, the company arranged to fake our deaths."

"I don't believe it."

"Don't then. I don't really care. But I saw the reports. We all had the kind of accident that doesn't leave a body. I heard from a guard I bribed that my funeral was nice."

Funeral? No. It couldn't be. One of the things Riley had held on to, hoped for once they got rescued, was eventually reuniting with her family. She shook her head. "I refuse to be dead. I'll find a way to get back home and show my family that I'm still alive. Then, we'll—"

"You'll what?" Carmen scoffed. "Stupid girl. You were never meant to return. The company covered its tracks well. If you try and go back, they'll just kill you, for real this time. And if you contact anyone you knew, they'll kill them too."

"But that's insane. They can't get away with this. I'm a civilian. I have rights."

"Not anymore, and they've already gotten away with it. So deal with it."

Incredulous, it took Riley a moment to sputter, "Deal with it? I'm just supposed to forget I had a life and a family? Just start over wherever it is we're going?" Doing who knew what. Living who knew how.

"We've been given a second chance. You want to fuck it up pining after something you can never have again, go ahead. I, for one, am thankful to be alive."

"For now. We're not free though. We're at the mercy of the cyborgs."

Carmen rolled her shoulders. "I'll admit the situation is not ideal. These cyborgs are a cold lot, some of them at least. But they're a heck of a lot better than the company. Better lovers too."

Riley's jaw dropped. "You've…you've had sex with one?"

"Sex is too mild a word. The man's a machine, and I don't mean that in a bad way. I've never had so many orgasms in a row. Smith is a master when it comes to playing my body, and even better, he can go at it for hours."

"Sounds chafing."

Husky laughter bubbled from Carmen. "Don't knock it until you try it."

Much as Riley wanted to deny she'd have sex with their cyborg captors, she couldn't help but recall how she'd pictured it with a certain big fellow. "I've got to go." Go find Aramus and ask him if it was true she could never go home. Find her room before she did something stupid such as seduce

Aramus and see if Carmen spoke the truth about cyborgs being masters of the climax.

Caught up in her thoughts, she didn't look before stepping into the hall and only narrowly avoided colliding with a stranger.

Riley caught herself and mumbled, "Sorry. I wasn't paying attention."

"Stupid cunt."

What? Casting her gaze up, she met the angry glare of a woman with short, spiked hair and a sneer on her lips. Recognizing the expression on the stranger as one stewing for a fight, Riley quickly determined that another apology seemed the wisest choice. "I'm sorry."

"Fe-fucking-fi-fucking-fo-fucking-fum. I smell me a human who needs to meet my fist."

While a part of Riley wanted to point out how poorly the last bit rhymed, self-preservation kicked in and told her to move her ass lest the punch aimed her way put a serious dent in her skull. With a squeak, she ducked. The deadly projectile narrowly missed her face and smashed into the wall behind her with enough force to leave a pockmark in the panel. *Ooh, that would have hurt.*

Whirling, she went to duck back into the common room, but the woman gripped the back of her jumpsuit and threw her sideways. Riley hit the wall with a cry and winced. Staggering from the impact, she didn't wait to see if the woman was done but pivoted on her heel, only to run into Aramus, who'd suddenly appeared.

His big, brawny arm curled around her as he snapped, "What the hell is going on? Why are you attacking my prisoner?"

"She's human," said the tough-looking female with a glare in her direction. "Isn't that enough reason? Of all the cyborgs on board, I'd expect you to understand."

"She's under our protection."

"She worked for them, which makes her a threat."

"Threat of what? Stomping on our toes? It's the only thing she can reach."

Another time, Riley might have taken offense and spoken up, but given the vicious-looking woman in front of her, whose orb-like eyes and words pegged her as a cyborg, she thought it prudent to stay silent. She also thought it best to take cover, and the best spot was behind Aramus. It would take more than one cyborg girl to get past him. She hoped.

"Why do you defend her?"

"I'm not. I thought I made myself clear in the last ship-wide memo that no one was to harm them."

He did? Riley relaxed a bit at the revelation.

It seemed, though, the other woman wasn't as crazy about his decree. "That was before you set them free to roam. Are you defective? All cyborgs know humans can't be trusted. Even the little ones."

Someone had anger issues. Then again, so did Riley. The only difference was she didn't blame a whole race for them. "I won't hurt you," she ventured. "Heck, I'm the person who can't even kill a fly."

"No one gave you permission to speak," yelled the female with a lunge.

Riley squeaked and dug deeper into Aramus's back, his big body a solid presence she trusted. How ironic, given the situation.

*

Aramus felt the little human press herself against his back. At least she had the common sense to seek shelter from the visibly pissed unit before him. "You're frightening her." And for some reason, he didn't like it.

"So what? She should be frightened. She should tremble and beg my forgiveness."

"Why? Did she harm you personally?" he asked.

"Not yet, but who the fuck knows what weapons she might hide? Or what codes she has stored in her head, waiting to be unleashed to turn us into her little fucking puppets?"

Shit, is this how I sound? Paranoid and irrational? Aramus might own arrogance in spades, but even he could hear echoes of himself in the hate-filled speech of the cyborg bristling before him. It was like looking in a mirror, if the mirror reflected attitude. On the one hand, it sounded badass; on the other, he could see the inanity, especially with the so-called vicious human cowering against his spine, the sharp scent of her fear displeasing him.

"You're safe now, Unit D802."

"Don't call me that. I have a name. Deidre."

"I'm sorry. I was not aware you'd chosen one."

"I didn't. Aphelion found it in my files. It is the name my mother chose for me before the humans stole me and changed me."

"When we return to our home world, Einstein will rid your BCI of the memory blocks."

"I am not sure I want to recall my human years."

"That is your choice. And, it should be noted, not all of us are capable of remembering. I, for example, know only what I've read in my file." Along with random snippets, most from the time when he was apprehended and the rage and injustice. Of his former family and life…only a blank spot remained.

"How long until we get to the cyborg home planet?"

"That is classified information." He changed the subject. "Are you in this part of the ship for a purpose?"

"Yes. I volunteered to aid with the injured cyborg. As I am not cleared yet for shipboard duties, I am good for little else."

"You know why we can't allow you access to our command center or engines."

"Yes," Deidre bit out through gritted teeth. "Because you fear a hidden bomb in my programming. And you wonder why I think the human should die."

He got tired of arguing with the female because cyborg or not, his sympathy only went so far. "It won't be long before you are cleared for duty and your mind set free. But, in the meantime, I am commander of this ship, which means you obey my fucking rules, and my rules state no killing of humans unless I sanction it." Especially not the little one at his back. If anyone got to kill her for getting under cyborg skin, it should be him, right after he figured out what it was about her that disturbed his usually well-balanced equilibrium.

With a growled, "Watch your back, human," Deidre stalked off.

Riley stepped away as he turned to glare down at her.

"Thank you," she murmured.

"Don't. I can understand where she's coming from. If it weren't for orders, you probably wouldn't be standing here."

He could tell his words startled her as her gaze flew upward to meet his. "You're not like her. You wouldn't just kill me."

"I would and could." He had in the past.

"I don't believe you." She stepped closer, into his personal space, close enough that an invisible current passed between them, rousing his cock. Why was he not surprised it disobeyed his order to stand down?

"Why the fuck do you persist in thinking I'm some nice guy? I'm not."

"No, you're not, but you're not completely without a heart like you'd make everyone believe." She placed a small hand on his arms, which he'd crossed over his chest. The simple touch burned him.

"I am worse than you can imagine. I've done things, bad things, and enjoyed it."

"Revenge is often like that."

How dare she seem understanding? "I'd wipe your planet out if someone gave me a nuke."

"Would you really?"

"In a second."

"That seems extreme."

"That's me. If the dead could speak, they'd tell you to fear me."

She shook her head. "If you're trying to scare me off, it won't work. I don't fear you. I see a man who is angry and hurt at the hand fate dealt him. I think you use violence and outrageous threats as a way of dealing with it."

"What are you now, my fucking shrink?"

"I'm trying to be your friend."

"I don't need your friendship." What he needed was her naked using her mouth for things other than talking.

"Actually, I think you do. I also think you need to let some of your anger go. What happened to you was horrible. They had no right. No one has the right to take your freedom and choices away. But you can't blame an entire race for the actions of a few."

"Why not?"

"That would be like me saying all cyborgs are psychos."

"Haven't you read the news? We are," he said in a mocking tone.

"Stop it. Stop trying to make yourself out to be something worse than you are. I get it. You're badass. I understand you want to punish someone. To make the pain go away. Well, so do I. I want to kill that prick Dennison who used to slap me around for no reason other than he could. I want to punch the guards who used to bring me food and spill it so they could laugh as I ate it from the dirty floor because I was so damned hungry. It's normal to want revenge on those who hurt us. What's not normal is refusing to acknowledge not everyone is like that."

"You have the names and faces of the people who wronged you. I don't."

"But you know I wasn't part of it."

"So you say."

"Do I look like someone who would hurt you?"

Hadn't she already by making him question his reason for being? By upsetting his carefully ordered world? "I don't trust you." Just like he didn't trust himself around her.

"Of course you don't because you don't know me. Give me a chance. Let me show you that not all humans are bad." Their eyes locked. He didn't move away as she lifted herself on tiptoe, not high enough to reach his lips, so she had to settle for brushing her mouth across his chin.

He shuddered. Tried to hold himself in check and not give in to her seductive allure. But he couldn't help but recall the doctor's orders, orders he'd decided to ignore, orders that plagued him, orders, which as a cyborg, he felt compelled to obey. Or at least that was his excuse when, with a groan, he caught her around the waist and lifted her so their lips could meet.

Once again all rational thought left his mind at their embrace, all but one. *I need a bed.* Or a room. Somewhere private where he could treat the ailment causing him to malfunction.

How they made it to her quarters he couldn't have said. He must have carried her because she clung to him and not once did their lips separate. They stumbled into the small space, the door sliding shut behind them, enclosing them and hiding his shameful desire from the cyborgs aboard.

With deft hands, he stripped her jumpsuit from her, eager to touch the skin he'd watched on camera. He couldn't wait to explore the curves that taunted his every waking and sleeping moment. She lay on her bed for him, her eyes half shut with passion, her lips swollen from his kiss, her skin flushed a rosy pink. He stored the image in his databanks, a snapshot of what a woman who truly desired him looked like. He'd never seen anything more beautiful.

But he wasn't here to admire. He was here to fuck. And taste. And touch.

It took him but a moment to kick off his boots and shed his clothes, torturous seconds where she watched him, burned him with her ardent gaze. Never before had he swelled so thick, felt so out of control, so needy…

Pinning her hands over her head, asserting his control of a situation that seemed determined to spiral out of his control, he fell upon her, his lips coasting the velvety smoothness of her skin. He nibbled on erect nipples, taut buds, which, when tugged, caused her to emit wondrous moans. The thigh he inserted between her legs pressed against her moist core, the heat and wetness of it causing his erection to jerk in anticipation. Having never fucked a human before, and with no past recollection of doing so, he couldn't believe the difference in texture from the droids he'd previously used. There was no comparison really. The real thing, the pliant flesh, the silky texture, the scent, all combined into a heady mixture that made him forget about control. The only thing he knew, and wanted, was to bury his cock.

Heaving himself over her, he kept her arms pinned over her head as he thrust into her. She gasped, and her gaze widened.

For a moment, rationality peeked its head. "Did I hurt you?"

"No. Just took me by surprise. You are a tad bit…large."

He was? He swelled at her words, and her breathing hitched. "You are small," he observed. Tight. Perfect.

"Not too small," she replied, her lips curling into a sensual smile for him. Her legs wrapped around his waist, drawing him deeper, and it was his turn to make a noise.

By all the nanos in his body, he'd never experienced such erotic decadence as being buried balls deep within her body. No. Wait. He spoke too soon. When he began to thrust, the strong suction of her sex, gripping and stroking him as he pushed in and out, that was the height of decadence.

Nirvana, however, was when her body bucked under him, her channel pulsing in waves, her climax drawing a cry amidst her panting breaths. With an incoherent sound of his own, Aramus joined her, his cock pulsing in time to her flesh-clinging waves, and for a moment, he closed his eyes and almost, almost recalled what it was to feel alive…and human.

Chapter Sixteen

Twice more they made love that night, each time a pulse-pounding, skin-heating, erotic encounter to put all of her past lovers to shame. Riley thanked the ounce of courage she'd found to make the first move. She'd gotten rewarded beyond her wildest expectation, which was why the emotional slap the next morning hurt so much.

It started with him dumping her on the floor in a tangle of blankets, her warm spot atop his chest rudely taken away. Sitting in the mess of sheets, she blinked at him, assuming an accident, only to see him, his face grim and closed off as he sat on the edge of her bed pulling on his trousers then his boots.

Somehow I don't get the feeling I'm getting an apology. "Is something wrong?" she ventured as she clasped the sheet to her breasts. Never mind the fact he'd seen and caressed it all, she needed a shield, even a fabric one.

"No."

"Then why do you seem so angry?"

"This is how I always look."

No, it wasn't. She'd seen a softer side to him, felt it and tasted it. "Are you going somewhere? Is the ship all right?"

"There is nothing wrong."

"Then why are you in such a hurry to leave?" she asked, irritation coloring her tone. He seemed prepared to ignore her as he stood. Like hell. She jumped to her feet and blocked his path to the door.

"I have duties to attend to."

"When will I see you again?"

And here came the second blow. "You won't."

"Excuse me?"

"Is your hearing defective? I have a ship to run. I won't be back."

Anger—mixed with shame at her stupidity—burned like acid in her stomach. "You used me."

"We used each other."

"So last night meant nothing?"

"We copulated."

"I thought it was more than that. I thought we connected."

"We did. My cock fit well in your pussy. But that's all it was. Sexual relief."

She hit him, as if her small fist could hurt. "You fucking used me for sex."

"What else did you expect?"

Something more than his callous disregard. "I expected a little respect."

"You are a human."

"Your point being? Despite your attempts to pretend you're not, half of you is as well. And, even if you weren't, it's not too much for me to expect some level of respect or courtesy. We were intimate. I don't just have sex with anybody."

"Then that is your problem. I never made any declarations. I had a need, and you were willing to accommodate."

She could hardly believe the coldness, the unfeelingness of his answer. "You asshole."

"Name calling is uncalled for."

"Oh, I'd say it's well deserved, you fucking prick." She pummeled him, unable to stop, her anger overwhelming even common sense.

It had no effect; he was done talking. He set her aside, her feeble blows of no account, and left her to her angry sobs of shame as she realized he'd spoken the truth. He didn't care.

Way to showcase our differences. Maybe he is only a machine because only something with no feelings could so callously treat what we shared together as nothing. But she, on the other hand, was all too human, and his rejection hurt.

How could I have been so stupid?

Sure, he'd never claimed he cared for her or made any promises. Still though, she'd asked him to trust her, to let her prove herself. She'd done so in the only way she knew how, by giving herself to him, by showing him pleasure. Apparently he'd not understood the gift she'd given him. Couldn't understand because he didn't remember what it was like to be human.

Riley sighed. Had she really expected to magically cure Aramus of his trust issues with great sex? He'd had years to develop and stew in his anger. How could she so foolishly think one night of pulse-pounding action would take away all his memories?

Seen from that perspective, it was hard to stay mad at him. She felt sorry instead, sorry that he couldn't let go of his past and hatred. She'd just have to try harder.

But how, when he claimed he didn't want to see her again?

We'll just see about that, Mr. Grumpy, because tenacity should have been my middle name.

*

Aramus had never felt more human and, at the same time, inhuman, as when he left Riley, her eyes welling with moisture. What else could he do though?

He'd done as the doctor ordered. He'd fucked her. Fucked Riley just like he'd imagined, and it proved more incredible than even he had hypothesized. So incredible he'd done it several times over the course of the night. Wanted to do it again this morning when he awoke, as a matter of fact. It became an almost imperative need when he'd discovered her splayed across his chest, her cheek against his skin, her head tucked under his chin, her hand over the spot where his organic heart used to reside.

He'd stroked a hand down her back, listening to her breath, so utterly content, and at peace. Even—gasp—happy, because of a human.

As soon as he'd recalled who she was, what she represented, he'd experienced a minor meltdown. Not a circuit board blowout or a silicone chip failure, but an emotional one. Utterly unacceptable.

I am a cyborg. I am a machine. I don't get fucking sappy. I don't admire sleeping women. I don't cuddle. And I definitely don't fucking care!

So why did he feel like such an asshole as he stomped away from Riley? Why did he want to go back and ask her forgiveness? Promise her he'd never hurt her again?

"Aramus, why do you look like someone shoved a—"

A fist shot sideways shut Xylo's fat mouth and started the brawl he needed to expend some pent-up tension. Fifteen minutes of tussling later, with a broken nose—number two hundred and thirty seven by his count—he sat in the medical bay, shoulders slumped as MJ popped the bent appendage back into place.

"Care to explain why you felt a need to pound your head of security's head off the floor?" MJ asked as he shone a light in his eyes, checking his retinas for damage. Xylo had landed a few solid punches, and Aramus saw the world in triplicate for a few minutes after the fight.

"This is your fault. I did what you told me. I fucked the human."

"I take it the experience left you feeling dissatisfied, hence your anger at a passing shipmate."

"No. I enjoyed it. All three times."

"But?" MJ drew out the word, waiting for more.

"But I wanted more." Wanted to hear her soft cries of pleasure as he thrust into her and feel her fingers digging into his shoulders, her breath hot against his lips. Closing his eyes and willing the images away didn't stop them.

"I take it the human couldn't handle your ardor given her frail nature and said no when you asked for more sex."

"Not exactly." He had a feeling Riley would have welcomed his touch. Actually, he knew she would have. Or had. After his actions, he doubted she would even want to speak to him. He'd acted like a jerk. She probably hated him now, which was as it should be, so why did the thought fill him with dissatisfaction?

"There is an expression on earth about people who don't volunteer information to those trying to help them. It goes, 'like pulling teeth'. Except, in your case, I am going to start removing body parts if you don't talk. I can't help you if I don't know the problem."

"Touch any body parts and I'll remove your arm and beat you with it."

"I'd like to see you try." MJ glared.

Aramus held in a sigh. While MJ was usually benign in nature, truth was their part-time doctor was a trained killer and a big fucking bastard who towered over even Aramus. In a head-to-head match, things could get dicey.

"I'm waiting, soldier. Spill your guts before I rip them out."

"Fine. You want the sordid details, here they are. I'm turning into a defective shadow of myself. I fucked Riley. I made her scream in pleasure. I shot like a bullet from a gun. Had the time of my fucking life, and then we goddamned fell asleep cuddling.

Fucking cuddling!" he yelled. "It's fucking emasculating. No, worse than that because I did it with a goddamned human. And I want to do it again. With her." Aramus waited for the derisive sneer, the disdain at his mental failing, the derogatory comments about being a human lover, one of those who slept with the enemy and liked it. It was what he would have done.

MJ did none of those things. He shrugged. "I don't see the problem."

"Did you not hear a fucking word I said?"

"I did. I heard you enjoyed yourself and that you like her.

"I. Don't. Want. To. Like. Her." He uttered it through gritted teeth, every word a lie.

"Well, apparently you do, else we wouldn't be having this conversation. I don't see what the big deal is. So what if she's human? Half of you is as well."

"Less than half. And I prefer to pretend it's not there."

MJ threw his hands up. "I give up. You are a stubborn prick. No. Worse than a prick, you're a racist."

"It's not racist to hate the people who hurt me."

"The military and the company did this to you. Not Riley. Not the majority of humans. Just two very specific groups. When are you going to get it through your thick metal head that hating all humans, in the long run, won't do you any good? Like it or not, we'll always have to deal with them. We'll always be connected to them."

"Not if I kill them all."

"And now you're being irrational. Maybe you are defective, because when it comes to logic and blaming the right people, you're not thinking clearly. Now if you're done being an asshole, I've got better things to do, like trim my toenails."

"Our nanos control their growth."

"It's called an excuse to leave you before your paranoid ramblings send me over the edge and I turn you into scrap metal art."

MJ stalked off, and Aramus glared at his retreating back. *Damned human lover. A true cyborg would understand.*

A wheezing laugh came from the bed in the corner where Avion propped himself into a sitting position. "Talk about entertainment."

"How much did you hear?"

"Enough to know MJ is right. You are an idiot."

"Not you too. Of all people, I would have thought you'd take my side, given your experience at their hands."

"Certain hands. Not all the humans I came in contact with were out to hurt me. Many even disagreed with my treatment. Not that it did them any good. The sadistic ones were in control, so I usually never saw the kinder ones again."

Aramus couldn't believe what his auditory organs were hearing. "Are you trying to tell me you don't hate and resent humans for their treatment?"

"Oh, I hate some of them. There are quite a few I'd love to get my hands on so I could torture them slowly, listening to them scream as I tear them apart limb from limb. But, unlike you, I'm not so bitter that I can't realize they are only a few, and, if their actions were known, even humans would shun them and take them to task for their actions."

"Good for you. I am not so forgiving."

"Then I feel sorry for you. You can't live your life hating who you are."

"I don't dislike myself. I hate humans." It sounded childish even to his ears, but he still stubbornly said it.

"Where is the logic behind that? Hate those deserving of it. Not those who've done you no harm. From the sounds of it, Riley likes you, even if you're a bigoted idiot."

His heart sped up at Avion's suggestion that Riley liked him. He regulated it back to a normal level. "I don't care what she thinks. I refuse to like her."

"Then don't. She's probably better off without you anyhow. Once we get to our home planet, you won't have to concern yourself with her anymore. Given the shortage of women, I'm sure someone will woo her into becoming his partner."

Riley with another cyborg? What? Like fuck! Anger seethed in him at the very thought. Uh-oh. He wasn't so far gone to not realize what he felt. Jealousy. Just another defect to lay at her feet. *She just keeps bringing out the worst in me, the human I've tried to keep locked away. I have to get rid of her.* "She's not going to our home world."

"Why not? I thought that was the plan."

"Not anymore." Because several things had occurred to him. One, their colony was rather small, which meant he'd run into her—and probably continue to lust after her. Seducing her wasn't an option; he didn't want people to know his shameful secret. Two, he didn't know if he could control himself if he saw her in the arms of another. Just the thought had his blood pressure ignoring his orders to calm the fuck down. And three, he didn't know what the third fucking reason was, other than he had to get rid of her, and since he couldn't bloody kill her—even if it was the most efficient course of action—then the only option left was to dump her and the other humans, under the guise, of course, of keeping his brethren safe. To admit he'd gotten rid of them so he wouldn't have to face a certain female just wasn't to be borne.

"We've got the information we need. The humans serve no purpose and have no value. Not to mention they pose a security risk. There's a way station for fueling in the Milky Way. I'll deposit them there."

"To do what?"

"Be with their kind."

"What if the company finds them? They won't want them talking about their experience."

"Not my fucking problem." He'd warn them to keep their mouths shut. It would be up to them if they listened or not.

In the meantime, until he got them to the space station, he'd just have to stay away from Riley, and the temptation she posed.

Chapter Seventeen

After Aramus's callous dismissal, Riley felt more alone than ever. Even the other humans on board seemed to keep to themselves, with Percy barely saying two words when she ran into him, Carmen always running off doing who knew what—although Riley could imagine given the amount of cleavage showing and the smirk on her lips. Of the others, she didn't see a hair.

Given Aramus's views on humans, and those of Deidre's, she didn't bother engaging the other cyborgs in conversation. Why bother? She didn't need to hear how they hated her because of her human heritage too. A girl could only take so much. Yet, despite that, she craved companionship, which was why she ended up in the medical bay to visit the still comatose David.

"At least you can't ignore me," she said aloud as she sat at his bedside.

"But he also can't answer," quipped Avion from his corner.

"I'm sorry. I didn't mean to disturb you. I'll leave." She rose and headed to the door.

"Please don't. It's boring as hell here. I wouldn't mind some company."

"Really? You do know I'm *human*?" She stressed it, and he laughed.

"Oh I know. Trust me. I've heard all about it. You got under Aramus's skin in a bad way."

"Well, eeeeexcuuuse me. If I'd have known what a jerk he would turn out to be, I would have stayed far away." Aramus seemed to have no problem keeping his distance. How was she supposed to change his mind and get him to trust her if she couldn't even see him?

"Yeah, his actions are pretty hard to defend, but I can understand."

"Really? Because I don't. I mean I get how cyborgs must be angry. You were dealt a crappy hand. You especially, from the looks of it. Yet, he has to know not all humans are like that. I'm not."

"I think deep down he knows this, but he's lived with his anger for years now. It was the only thing he had once he was liberated. Unlike some of us, he's got no memories of his past or family. No recollection of what it's like to care. He probably wouldn't recognize it if it slapped him upside the head."

Or slept with him. "So he's going to live his whole life hating an entire race for the actions of a few?"

"That's one possibility."

"What's the other?"

"Maybe he just needs the right incentive, or person, to show him the error in his thinking."

"Not me."

"Why not? From what I hear, you both shared an, um, how to say this delicately, intimate moment."

She snickered. "You can say it. We had sex, and it meant nothing to him. He was just taking care of a need." Aramus's callous dismissal of the night they'd spent together rankled still, even days later.

"Oh, it was more than that. Trust me. I know him. There is no way he would have slept with you otherwise. Aramus is a very controlled being. He never lets his emotions, or even his bodily needs, sway him from being the perfect cyborg soldier. Until he met you."

"Ha. I find that hard to believe." Every encounter with him, except for their very first, ended in either a kiss or more.

"Believe it. The fact he has so little control around you has him scared. He fears you."

She couldn't control her laughter. "That big tough guy fears me? That's priceless."

"He fears losing hold of his hatred and allowing himself to care. To maybe acknowledge that not all humans need culling and that there is more humanity in him than he wants to admit. He sees emotions as a weakness."

"Why are you telling me all this? I can't help but think Aramus would be pissed if he heard you talking to me like this."

"Oh, I'm sure he is."

"Is? You mean he's here?" She peered around. "I don't see him."

"He's not here physically, but I'll wager he's listening. I'll bet he's always watching where you're concerned."

He was? Maybe not all hope was lost. "You're going to get yourself in trouble."

"Aramus won't hurt me. Yell loudly, maybe, but he won't damage me."

"Okay, since you say you know him so well, what do you suggest I do?"

"Force him to care."

She snorted. "How? It's not like I can get him in a head lock and noogie him until he cries uncle."

"Damn. I'd love to see that. Heck, I'll even hold him down while you do it. Just do me a favor and wait until Einstein fits me with some new eyes before you do."

"Deal. But you still haven't said how I can get him to care when I haven't even seen him. He's kept himself hidden in the forbidden parts of the ship."

Avion shrugged, and his lips tilted into a mischievous grin. "So make him come to you."

"How?"

"You need to do something that will evoke a strong enough emotional response that he won't be able to help himself. Like making him jealous."

Pretend to like another cyborg? She vetoed that. Not only did it seem too calculating, but, if Avion was right, Aramus could severely damage one of his friends. "That seems too underhanded."

"What if he thinks you're in danger?"

Put herself in harm's way? And what if Avion was wrong? She could get hurt. Nope. She wasn't that desperate. She shook her head before she realized he couldn't see her reply. "Not happening either."

"Since he can't seem to resist you, make him horny."

How could she make him lust after her if he wasn't around? Or did he constantly watch her as Avion suggested? Only one way to find out.

"You've given me a lot to think about."

"Don't think too long. I'd hate for you both to miss out."

"What are you implying?"

"Nothing. Just think about what I said."

She would. She did. And then she acted. If her life as a prisoner had taught her anything, it was that life was too short to sit waiting for someone else to act. She'd gotten a second chance. It was up to her not to waste it.

Chapter Eighteen

What is she up to now? Aramus wondered as Riley entered her quarters and paced. She seemed to be having a discussion with herself, a silent one that had her alternately frowning and biting her lip, as if she tried to come to a decision. He wondered what had perturbed her.

Despite recognizing the weakness of his actions, Aramus couldn't help but keep tabs on Riley. As usual, as soon as he hit his quarters, his camera feeds were tuned in to her. He'd observed her moroseness, seen the hope in her eyes when she heard a heavy footstep in the hall, only to lose it when she saw who approached.

She misses me. A theory confirmed after her talk with Avion. Damn the cyborg for telling her Aramus spied on her. It was humiliating in the extreme that he couldn't help himself, but even more so to know Avion had guessed his weakness. He almost marched down to the sick bay to give the injured unit a good yelling at, maybe a shake and rattle of his obviously loose bolts, but to act in any way meant he'd have to admit he spied, which created a conundrum. He played it cool—which didn't sit well. He really preferred to hit and kill things when perturbed.

Thankfully the torture would end soon. They'd reach the way station he aimed for in the next few days. He could hold out that long. He could resist the temptation. He could—

What the fuck is Riley doing? It started with her unzipping her jumpsuit, which in and of itself wasn't unusual, but the slowness she did it with, the sensual shrug of a shoulder to send the fabric sliding down one arm then the other, that was unusual.

The garment fell to her waist, baring her tank top-clad torso. Gripping the jumpsuit, she wiggled it over her hips, those perfect, voluptuous hips, and down creamy thighs before letting it go to pool at her feet. Dressed only in the white shirt and underpants, she stepped out of it, and he switched cameras, expecting to see her enter the washroom for a shower, the only reason she usually undressed in the daytime. And, yes, he fully admitted he was a defective bot for spying on her. He knew that and knew there was a name for his actions, voyeur. It didn't stop him from watching…and enjoying.

His cock grew fat with anticipation. It did so enjoy the sensual visual of her when she bathed, but on this occasion, she never entered the small washroom. Odd. Aramus flipped the view back to her room to find Riley nude and stretched out on her bed, legs splayed, exposing her pink sex. By all the nanos in his system, she presented a visually stimulating sight. He memorized and saved it to his memory banks.

But hold on a moment. Why was she gripping her breasts and squeezing them? To what purpose did she roll her nipples between her fingers until they stood erect and begging for a mouth—*my mouth*—to suck them?

The answer stunned him. *She's masturbating.*

More than ever, voyeuristic tendency or not, he knew he should turn the camera feed off. This was wrong. So wrong. So fucking tempting…

He forced himself to stay seated, even as he remained riveted by the unfolding scene. Frozen, as if stunned by a Taser, he watched as Riley caressed a body he couldn't forget. A body he wanted to touch again.

He could have fought through the allure she presented and jerked off as she touched herself if she'd not crooked her finger and looked right at the camera. Right at him. Then she mouthed his name.

Aramus didn't recall rising from his seat, leaving his room, or how he ended up outside her door. As if on autopilot, he went to her, her unspoken command obeyed by the soldier in his pants. Oh, who was he trying to fool? He went to her because he wanted her and missed her. He went to her because she made him feel, even if he didn't always like what those feelings meant. *I'm here because this is where I want to be. Where I belong.*

The door made only the slightest of sounds as it slid open, allowing him entrance. He stepped in, and it closed behind him, giving them privacy. His gaze immediately flicked to the bed, where he expected at least a token of surprise. But he'd not misread her invitation on the camera. Far from startled, Riley greeted him with a sensual smile.

"About time," she murmured, her voice husky. "I thought I was going to have to finish by myself."

"What are you doing?" His question came out harsher than he meant, raw with the hunger he'd suppressed.

"Trying to get your attention."

"Why?"

She licked her lips, a pink flick of her tongue that did nothing to help his pulsing erection. "You've been avoiding me."

"I was doing my job."

"Ah yes, taking care of your ship and crew." She let out a low laugh. "Such a good cyborg. But you forgot one thing."

"No I haven't."

"Yes you have. As part of this ship and one of your passengers, you've neglected something I need."

"According to records, you've been cared for. Food. Accommodations. Clothing. What else do you require?" A part of him knew her answer, expected it, but a selfish part of him wanted her to say it.

"I need you."

His eyes closed as her words washed over him, warming him not physically but mentally. "You don't know what you're asking."

"Don't I?"

"I'm cyborg."

"And?"

"I can't give you anything more than my body."

"I wasn't asking for anything else."

Even he could hear the unspoken "for now". "Why me?" Why not one of the others? Why did she want him? Why would she choose him knowing his ornery nature? Knowing his opinion on her kind?

"Because I can't help myself. I want you, Aramus. You and only you. You desire me too. Don't deny it. If you didn't, you wouldn't be here right now."

"I hate this weakness."

"It's not weakness to want to feel."

With his eyes still closed, he didn't see her rise from the bed, but he heard it then felt it as she looped her arms around his body and leaned up to nibble the edge of his chin.

"I am defective," he whispered.

"No, you're mine."

And with that possessive claim, he could hold back no longer. Groaning in surrender, his arms came around her, crushing her to him as he lifted her to mash his mouth against hers in a fiery kiss.

She clung to him, meeting his fierce embrace and adding to it with her lithe tongue. How could he have thought he could resist her? She was his weakness. The one human who could bring him to his knees. And to his knees he dropped, dragging her with him, peppering her with kisses, trying to reach all her sensitive spots, behind the lobe of her ears, the pulse in her neck.

Arching, she threw her head back, giving him access, making herself vulnerable before him. Forget the fact a bed was readily accessible only a few feet away. He couldn't stop his sensual exploration of her body, especially when her hands tugged at his clothing. He aided her in shedding his shirt and unbuttoning his pants. He cursed when he had to let go of her to remove his boots and bottoms, a temporary reprieve she used to crawl up onto the bed, splayed out across the cover, an erotic invitation he could not resist, no matter how much his computer programming screamed danger.

He'd always liked to live on the edge.

Between his legs, his erection pulsed, and his balls hung heavy. The sweetness of her arousal perfumed the air, a decadent scent more deadly than any military gas. With her legs spread, he could clearly see her glistening sex. He couldn't help but touch her there, feel her desire on his fingers. She was so ready for him, and they'd barely just begun.

He dropped to his knees once more, a supplicant before her fleshly altar. Gripping her thighs, he tugged her until her ass rested on the edge of the bed, her legs draped over his shoulders, putting her in a perfect position for his mouth.

Since his rebirth, Aramus had partaken of many foods, some considered delicacies, some sweet, some tart, but none, nothing he recalled, tasted as good as her pussy when he licked it. Her honey coated his tongue, her arousal an ambrosia made for him. He ate like a man starving, nibbling and sucking, tongue penetrating and exploring. He heard her crying out his name, begging for more, her breathing irregular, all audible signs that she enjoyed his decadent meal of her flesh. When she came, he almost came with her, so awed was he at the way her body bucked with the strength of her orgasm, how her sex convulsed at the peak of her climax.

It was fucking beautiful. And still she begged him for more.

"Take me, Aramus," she pleaded. "I need you. God, how I need you."

And I need her.

He tugged her back onto the bed, keeping her legs spread so he could settle himself between them. The tip of his cock rubbed against her swollen clit. Riley made an inarticulate sound as she arched, trying to draw him into her body. But she'd just come, and while still aroused, he retained enough wits to know she needed more if he wanted her to come again. Which suited him fine because her arching drew attention to her luscious breasts.

Braced on his forearms, he continued to rub his swollen head against her clit while he leaned down and captured a swollen tip in his mouth. He sucked, and she grabbed his head, not at all put off by his metal plate, and pushed her breast farther into his mouth. As if he'd let her dictate his actions in bed. He pulled back so he could graze his teeth over her erect nipple. Riley panted and thrashed. She definitely liked that. Aramus swirled his tongue around her taut nub before applying suction to her breast.

Moisture gushed from her sex, soaking his already lubed head. Close. She was so close to being ready for him again. He switched his attention to her other breast and gave it the same attention, to her moaning delight.

Forget sliding his cock against her clit. He pushed the fat head of his cock into the entrance of her sex. Tight, so wickedly, fucking tight. Perfect. *Mine.*

With that possessive thought running in a loop, he thrust, sinking deep into her velvety channel and couldn't help but moan at the exquisite feeling. Her slick muscles tightened like a vise around his dick, squeezing him tight, not wanting to let him go. Aramus almost lost it then and there. But he was a cyborg. He had more control. Barely.

Back he pulled, the suction of her sex reluctant to set his free. When only the head of his cock remained buried, he pushed himself as deep as he could, sheathing himself until his balls slapped up against her. Riley let out a high keening sound and clawed at his back. Aramus retreated and slammed back in, hard and deep. This time Riley let out a short scream. It seemed he'd found her sweet spot, and he took full advantage. With long, measured strokes, Aramus pushed in and then pulled out. Each jab struck her G-spot, her muscles flexing each time he hit. Tighter and tighter her channel squeezed until, with a loud scream, she exploded, her orgasm a wild, intense joining of their flesh that milked him. More than milked him, it stole all his control, and Aramus joined her in coming, so connected to her in that moment that he couldn't help himself from thinking, *I can never let her go.*

Chapter Nineteen

Holy smokes, she'd gotten more than she'd bargained for, in a good way. Aramus had come to her, torn by his desire, but also unable to resist. It made her melt inside to see the inner battle he fought, for once his expression not a guarded mask as desire fought with wariness…and wistfulness.

He wanted what she offered, but didn't trust it. In the end, he couldn't help himself. They made love. Wild, unbelievable love, and even when he came, shouting her name, his voice raw, he didn't forget about her. Instead of collapsing atop her—which would have probably crushed her to death—he remembered her more fragile human nature and rolled, keeping them connected, until he lay on his back with her splayed atop him.

Catching her breath, with her cheek against his skin, she noted something strange and couldn't help but ask, despite the intimate moment, "Why can't I hear your heart beat?"

"Because I don't have one."

The answer startled her enough that she pushed herself up so she could look at his face. "Excuse me? I thought I heard you say you didn't have a heart."

A crooked grin curled one corner of his mouth, softening the harsh lines of his face. "Your ears are functioning. I don't have a heart. One of my upgrades involved removing that particular organ and replacing it with a more efficient mechanical one."

"It pumps your blood? Keeps you alive?"

"Yes."

She sighed in relief. "Oh, thank god. For a minute there I thought I just had amazing sex with a dead guy."

"I would have thought my actions would have proven I was more than alive," was his wry reply.

A giggle slipped from her. "Sorry. It's just if you approach this from a logical standpoint, then, when you don't hear a heartbeat, it's because a guy is usually a vampire or a zombie."

"You are comparing me to a make-believe character?"

"It's not an insult. I love reading romances where vampires seduce the girl."

"Except, in this case, you seduced me."

"So I did." Riley grinned. "And, might I say, I'm glad I found the guts to do it."

"That would make two of us."

"You're not going to dump me on the floor now and run away, are you?"

For a moment, something passed across his face, regret, sadness, something else? But his words put her fears to rest. "No. For as long as we are stuck together on this ship, I won't avoid you."

Something about the phrasing of it bugged her, but she couldn't have said why. "Gee, how romantic."

"If you expect me to turn into a sappy, poetry-spouting idiot, then think again. I don't do flowery speeches. I don't give compliments. And I don't cuddle."

"Then what do you call what we're doing?" She wiggled atop him and arched a brow.

A slow, naughty smile stretched his lips. "Preparing for round two."

Aramus made love to her again, slowly and with reverence. He explored her body with his hands and mouth. For a man who professed he wouldn't compliment her, he gave lie to his words with the way he worshipped every inch of her, treating all of her body like a temple, with him as the devoted acolyte in charge of it.

She'd never felt more beautiful or desired. Several days they spent in bliss. The only time they separated was when he left to attend his duties on the bridge. They ate in her room. Napped together. Bathed together and made love countless times.

But they didn't just make love. They also spoke, she of the life she used to lead while Aramus, with a lot of prodding, told her of his liberation and how he came to sentience. She could tell how the experience had scarred him and how he resented the fact that, unlike some of the other cyborgs, he could remember almost nothing of his past. She heard the affection in his tone as he told her stories of others, his friends. She was fairly sure that Aramus, Mr. I-Don't-Feel-Anything, had no idea how his face lightened when he relayed some of the pranks and missions they'd done together. During all of their discussion, not once did he bring up his hatred of humans. She thought he was finally beginning to trust her. Thought he'd come to care for her.

How could I have been so wrong?

Chapter Twenty

I don't believe it.

"They're leaving." Even as she stared out the spaceport window, watching the *SSBiteMe* pull away from the docking area, she couldn't believe it. Aramus had dumped her. Dumped her as a lover, and so coldly, like she was an unwanted piece of cargo, and on a bloody space station in the middle of nowhere. *How could he abandon me?* She bit her lip, hoping the pain would keep the moisture welling in her eyes at bay.

"Well, at least they didn't k-k-ill us," Percy said.

Might as well have because it sure felt like she'd been stabbed in the heart.

Only Carmen didn't seem too shocked as she snorted. "Of course they didn't kill us. Cyborgs might call themselves machines and talk about how they are without emotion, but they're more human than they want to admit and subject to many of the same weaknesses. A true robot wouldn't have hesitated to terminate us so we couldn't tell anyone what we learned. But, apparently, they're not logical enough. They let their feelings rule," she sneered, not bothering to couch her usual disdain in a veneer of civility. "They were weak and let us go."

"It's not weak to have empathy," Riley answered. Although, according to Aramus, it was. Or at least that formed the basis of his logic and why he'd fled with his crew instead of dealing with the fact he felt something for Riley. *I know he cares for me.* She'd seen it too many times over the course of the past few days to doubt it, which made his abandonment without so much as a goodbye or chance to argue so much harder to bear.

"If you think that, then you're an idiot. Leaving loose ends is a failing, not a redeeming quality. No wonder the cyborgs failed as a project. The military should have burnt their ability to feel from their brains."

"Are you insane?" Riley couldn't help but exclaim. "Are you actually criticizing the fact they're capable of feeling? That they retained their humanity and that, despite the changes to their bodies, they're more than machines?"

"No, they're not. They're cyborgs. Built to serve mankind. The military and the company who developed the idea took flawed human beings, specimens who either gave back nothing to society or were injured in such a way as to pose a burden, and gave them a chance to be something more. Something better. What a shame they ended up such utter failures."

"How can you say that? You spent time with them. Hell, you were even sleeping with one."

"More than one, but that's neither here nor there. They made a mistake in leaving us here. In their shoes, I would have killed us all or kept us as tools."

"With that kind of reasoning, then you're no better than the monsters we escaped." And much more knowledgeable about the cyborgs than she'd formerly let on. It bothered Riley to know Carmen had lied, apparently about more than one thing, given her vitriolic diatribe. She wished she could tell Aramus. He'd probably want to question Carmen again, given this new insight. Just one problem. Aramus was gone, and she'd never speak to him again. *I guess it no longer matters.*

"Did I forget to mention I don't care about your opinion? As a matter of fact, I don't care for your presence. I'm out of here." Carmen whirled on her heel and strode across the mostly empty room that served as bar and restaurant for this section of the space station. At this late hour, it held nothing but a handful of patrons, lost in their thoughts as they nursed drinks and murmured quietly amongst themselves. They didn't spend more than a moment glancing at the drama unfolding in their corner.

Riley resisted a childish urge to give Carmen a single finger salute goodbye.

Percy, on the other hand, seemed perturbed at Carmen's departure. "Where are you g-g-going?"

"N-none of your d-d-d-damned business," Carmen mocked. "I've got better things to do than hang with you losers."

Bitch. Leave or stay, Riley didn't care. She'd not associated much with Carmen while on the cyborg ship, so she didn't really care what the woman did now that they'd achieved quasi freedom, especially given her rude remarks about their captors.

Maybe she's the smart one though. I don't see her mooning and moping about the fact her lovers ditched her. If only she could set aside her own emotions so easily. But the cranky cyborg had gotten under her skin.

Made her see the man who thought he couldn't care. Made her fall in love then left her with a broken heart, alone on a space station with no money and no way home.

What the hell am I supposed to do now? Call for help? Carmen's warning—was it only just over a week ago?—about not communicating with her family lest the company kill her, and them, echoed in her head. But if she couldn't contact them for a flight home, or even hitch a ride back to earth lest she trigger some kind of alert, what could she do?

Apparently, the uncaring cyborgs had made some accommodations. Rooms had been booked for each of them and paid through until the next month, so at least that took one dilemma out of the equation. They'd also been left enough credits to feed themselves and purchase some necessities, so she wouldn't starve or run around in the same pair of undies. Now if only she could figure out what to do with the rest of her life.

Which, as it turned out, might not last too long.

The attack occurred only hours after their arrival, hours she'd spent crying until she fell into an exhausted sleep. The station was invaded while she slumbered, and it seemed she wasn't the only one to miss it. No alarms rang. No premonitions warned her. However, it was pretty hard to ignore the hand clasped over her mouth or the gun held to her head when she blinked the sleep from her eyes.

"Don't fucking move or scream, or I'll blow your head off." In the dim light of her room, she could only nod as the intruder, clad in space riot gear—helmet, goggles, and spacesuit complete with air recycler—yanked her to her feet.

"Who are you?"

The blow to the back of her head sent her to her knees. "What part of keep fucking quiet did you not get?" Eyes stinging, noggin throbbing, she bit back a sob, lest the thug hit her again for not obeying. She'd forgotten what it was like to deal with jerks. Her time with the cyborgs had spoiled her, how ironic. "Get up, you stupid bitch, and move where I tell you. And I don't want to hear a fucking peep."

Thankfully, Riley had worn a T-shirt and track pants to bed because her attacker didn't give her time to dress, not even to slip on a pair of shoes before he marched her to the door. Into the hall they stepped, where more of the mercenaries clad in stealth gear waited. She noted Percy, his mouth clamped shut in a tight line, his hands bound and his eyes wide, in the grasp of another thug.

Icy fingers tickled her spine. Shit. This was so not good. Obviously, this was a targeted kidnapping, a belief reinforced when she saw Carmen exiting her room ahead of another soldier.

The other woman didn't appear flustered or surprised at all. As a matter of fact, she strode ahead of the accompanying kidnappers, a princess with attendants instead of a prisoner. Suspicion reared its ugly head. *Is Carmen in cahoots the mercs?* Surely not. But she daren't ask, not with Mr. Smack-Happy at her back.

"Is this all of them?" one of the thugs queried.

"Yes. These are the ones they wanted."
Who wanted?

Percy stupidly asked and got a slug to the gut for a reply. Riley decided she didn't need to know that badly. Eyes down, she stared at her bare feet and moved where they prodded. She wasn't about to test their patience by disobeying orders or attempting to escape. With these kinds of odds, even if she was a super healing cyborg, she'd hesitate to act. Suicide wasn't in her best interest.

Through the space station they wandered, the late hour meaning they traveled mostly in gloom as the lights of the facility were on nighttime mode, simulating the time zones back on earth. What surprised her was the lack of bustle and the quiet when they got to the docking area. Space ports, from what she knew, always had something happening, whether it was refueling, reloading, or maintenance, during off times. Then again, those things would be better accomplished by staff not slumped over their stations, dead or asleep; she couldn't quite tell.

The bodies ignobly splayed on the floor, on the other hand, in a chaotic half circle in front of the open door and ramp to a parked vessel, didn't need their puddles of congealing blood to announce violence had recently occurred.

Her sense of dread deepened.

She dragged her feet, yet that didn't halt the inevitable. A cuff upside the head, a gloved hand twisting in her hair, and a yank toward the opening in the spacecraft meant she had no choice. Sometimes it sucked being just a normal girl. What she wouldn't give for some super cyborg strength right about now. She was getting mighty tired of violent men dictating to her.

Once aboard, she wasn't surprised to see Dennison's sneering face. "Welcome back, Doctor. I hope you didn't think we'd abandoned you."

"A person can hope." And see that hope dashed.

"Once an employee of the company, always an employee."

"What does a girl have to do to get fired?"

The slap across her face rocked her and loosened a few teeth. Big surprise, Dennison still enjoyed smacking defenseless women around. Where was an unfeeling cyborg when you needed one?

"Mouthy bitch. It seems someone has forgotten her manners. No worries. I'll be by later to give you a refresher. Just as soon as we catch up with some machines who need to be reminded who is in charge."

"You'll never find them."

"Don't tell me you're rooting for the robots? Ah yes, I'd almost forgotten. According to my sources, you developed a fondness for one. Fucked him apparently."

How did he know? Who told him? She played dumb. "What are you talking about?"

"Oh, don't play stupid with me. I know all about your little fling with the ugly brute who now calls himself Aramus. Do you know, before the military drafted him, he used to be a homeless urchin? Begging on street corners. Petty theft. A few assaults. Such a prize."

"He's changed."

Dennison laughed. "I'll bet he has. And he has the company to thank."

"Don't you mean the military? I thought he was a soldier."

"He was. The military took him in and tried to make him into an obedient little soldier. But, as with many of his ilk, it failed. That's where the company stepped in. He was volunteered to the cyborg project."

"Volunteering implies choice."

"People like him don't deserve one. They're too stupid to do what needs to be done. That's why there are people like General Boulder to make those hard choices."

"And people like you?" She didn't say it nicely, but he smiled as if she'd paid him a compliment.

"Yes, like me. I saw the potential in him, in all that healthy, strong flesh. We gave him a third chance. A chance to become something greater than he was. A chance to serve. But, once a fuck-up, always a fuck-up."

"Aramus is a good man."

"Machine. You seem to forget that."

"You might have given him some electronic and metal parts, but he's still very much a man."

"Apparently, and quite the lover too judging by your defense of him. If I'd have known you were so desperate for male attention as to fuck even a robot, I would have rectified your problem, even if you're a little big for me. Never fear. Fat ass or not, I'll make sure you don't feel neglected this time round."

The sadistic gleam in his eyes let her know it wouldn't be a gentle experience. Rape never was. More than ever she wanted to scream and cry, but giving in to the terror coursing through her blood wasn't an option. She needed to remain alert and in control, lest she miss an opportunity to free herself from this nightmare. *Foolish hope because how do I expect to free myself from a spaceship?* Maybe she should hope for aliens to beam her aboard. Surely, their idea of probing was preferable.

"What, no tears? No begging to spare you? Or are you harboring a slim hope that your cyborg lover will rescue you?"

"Aramus and his crew are long gone. You'll never find them."

"Gone, but not lost." Dennison laughed. "I can see your confusion. Surely you didn't think we'd let you escape so easily? We had plans in place in case something like the cyborgs invading our installation happened. Actually we counted on it, as we required more specimens."

"You bugged us." Why did that not surprise her?

"And risk the cyborgs catching on? No. Nothing like that. But we did leave bait at the installation, which the stupid machines took."

She caught his implication. "One of the captives was a spy."

"Only one?" He laughed. "Foolish girl. We're not stupid enough to have only one. As a matter of fact, in spite of them dumping you and the others, they still have one on board. And they don't even know it. Don't even suspect."

"Who are the spies?"

"Does it really matter?"

"I want to know."

"Still stupid, I see," Carmen replied as she moved to stand beside Dennison and smiled up at him.

"You? But you slept with the cyborgs."

The Latina traitor shrugged. "Sex is sex. What better way to divert suspicion?"

"So who's the other one? David? The mute women?" Whom she'd never truly gotten to know and whom she'd not seen since their dumping on the station.

"Those expendables? Not likely. We've disposed of them now that we don't need them to camouflage our true spies."

"But that only leaves…" Oh, god. One of the cyborgs Aramus rescued was a traitor.

"The cyborgs they supposedly freed. Ironic, isn't it? The machines save other machines, acting on some weak morality that they need to rescue their kind, and yet that will be their downfall."

Oh, please don't tell me it's Avion. She'd grown to like the injured cyborg and couldn't picture him as a traitor. Not after the abuse he'd suffered. It would destroy Aramus if he ever discovered his friend had betrayed them. Or maybe Avion didn't know. Maybe he harbored a bug, or something, that made him an inadvertent spy. Whatever the case, it didn't bode well.

The engines purred to life under her feet as the craft prepared for flight.

"Enough spilling of secrets. Much as I've enjoyed our refreshing chat, it's off to your cell you go. Once we take care of the cyborg ship, we'll be on our way to your new home, with new test subjects."

"You mean new dead bodies."

"Only if we're unlucky. See, with the failure of human hosts to accept the DNA, we've opted to go in a different direction, one which we were about to begin when we were so rudely invaded and interrupted. But that turned out to be fortuitous. The new cyborgs I plan to capture will provide ample fodder for the next round of experiments, the nanos in their bodies hopefully the catalyst needed to accept and blend the alien DNA with human."

"For what purpose?"

"Wouldn't you like to know?" With a malicious grin, Dennison gestured to the guards behind her. This time when they clasped her arms, she fought. She couldn't go back to her cage, not knowing this time she wouldn't escape, that the entire time she'd enjoyed freedom it was but a sham. She couldn't go back to living like a victim.

But they paid no mind to her feeble kicks, thrashing, or hurled invectives. It took just one gun butt to the head for her to sink into blackness.

Chapter Twenty One

"What the fuck did you do?"

Aramus spared Avion only a quick glance before returning his stare to the screen before him and the stars whipping by as they sped away from the source of his malfunction. So far, distance wasn't providing the instant cure he'd hoped for. "Shouldn't you still be in bed?" he grumbled.

"I'm tired of lying around like some useless mannequin. Beside, when I heard the news, I had to come tell you in person what a fucking idiot you are."

"And how many walls did you dent on your way?" Because without his eyes and with his cyborg senses still refusing to function correctly, Avion was still very much an invalid.

"Who cares about some replaceable fucking panels? How could you just dump Riley like that?"

"I did what had to be done."

"No. You did the easy thing."

Easy? Exactly how was leaving Riley behind, considered easy? Aramus had fought an inner battle nonstop since he'd had her and the other humans escorted from the ship. He'd almost had to blind himself to prevent himself from checking the videos, fearful if he saw her reaction, he'd recant. "The humans were a security risk."

"To who?"

"All of us. Someone has been trying to send messages."

"And you traced it back to the captives?"

"Not exactly, but who else could it be?"

"Me. Deidre. Anyone on the crew. If you were so convinced one of them was a traitor why didn't you slap them into a cell and get them to confess? Or do what you usually do, execute them."

"I don't have to explain myself to you."

"Maybe not, but you will have to explain your irrational actions to Joe."

"I'll deal with Joe." Who would probably also call him a fucking idiot for dumping the company employees because he couldn't handle how one little female made him feel.

"I hate to interrupt your fascinating discussion," Aphelion interjected, "but I thought you might want to know that the space station we left the humans on was attacked."

"What the fuck do you mean the station got attacked?" An icy chill settled in Aramus, at odds with his usually high temperature.

Aphelion pointed to the SOS scrolling across his screen. "Not even four hours after we left, an unidentified craft docked and gassed the place with a sleeping agent."

"I thought all facilities had measures in place to prevent that kind of thing after the pirates adopted that tactic a few years back when they raided."

"They did, but only in the docking area itself. Those on guard in that area had masks on and weren't affected. They're also the ones who died. All who resisted were killed."

The coldness within Aramus deepened. "What were they after?"

"Here's the messed-up part. They were after the prisoners we dropped off. Nothing else."

His mechanical heart stopped beating for a millisecond. No. Fuck no. He'd feared as much as soon as Aphelion mentioned the raid. "They're all dead?"

"Not all. They killed the guy in the coma and the two mutes but seem to have abducted the others."

"They took Riley?"

"Riley, Carmen, and Percy."

He almost sighed in relief. *She lives.* "Are you sure?"

"It's what I just said, isn't it?"

Yes, but he needed to confirm before he did something irrationally rash. "We need to turn around."

"What for?"

"So we can go after that fucking ship."

"Again, I have to ask what for?"

"Are you being deliberately obtuse? To fucking save them, of course."

"I still don't get why. They are only humans," Aphelion mocked. "Isn't it you who always says, 'the only good human is a dead human'? Why should we bother helping them? If they want to kill each other off, then that's their business."

Aramus was less than impressed, even if it was true. "Since when are you such an asshole?"

"Me? I'm just repeating things I've heard you say in the past."

Fucking hell. Why did Aphelion have to choose now to listen to anything he said? "Well, that was before."

"Before what?"

Before he'd met a human who reminded him that not all of them were evil. Reminded him he was capable of caring and who liked him in return, even if he was an ornery asshole. "Forget what I've said. Since when does anyone listen?"

"Since you usually put us in a headlock and yell it at us until we cry uncle."

"Well, maybe I've changed my mind."

"You?" Avion, still present, snickered. "Since when does Mr. I-Wouldn't-Piss-On-A-Burning-Human suddenly give a fuck?"

Trust Avion to take over Seth's role in annoying the hell out of him and making him admit that perhaps he'd been wrong. "I do suddenly care, damn you. Is that what you want to fucking hear? I hate it, but I care. I should have not let my defective emotions cloud my judgment and left Riley there. Want to strip me of my command? Maybe mock me some more? I fucked up and now I need to fix it." He needed to get back there and save Riley before they hurt or killed her.

"You do realize she might already be dead?" Aphelion raised a valid point, one Aramus preferred not to dwell on because it chilled him to his core.

"No. She can't be." He couldn't help his frustrated roar or the fist he smashed against the metal post that served as a structural beam in the command center. It didn't hurt more than knowing he'd failed Riley. Because of his fear, he'd put her in danger, and yes, now that she was gone, perhaps forever, he could admit his fear. He should have listened to his friends, pushed past his own prejudice, and kept her at his side. *It wouldn't have killed me to admit I felt something for her, and I could have punched anyone out who dared make fun of me for it.* "She can't be dead." No logic backed his claim other than his own hope.

Avion tendered the hope Aramus needed. "Given the trouble they went through to get her back, not likely. If they were looking to silence her and the others, they would have executed them on the station or blown the damned place up."

"So you think she's intact?"

"Yes. For the moment. But the longer we wait to save her, the more time they have to change their minds or harm her."

"No!" Frustration and impatience did not mix well. Aramus needed something to kill. Right now. "We need to go after them. Fast."

"The good news is we don't have to go back and look for those responsible."

Aramus paused in his tantrum—which the steel support bore with dented grace—to glare at Aphelion. "I am not following your logic."

"We don't need to go back because, the bad news is, they're on our tail."

It didn't take a genius to figure out what that meant. There was only one way a ship could have been dispatched quickly enough to raid the way station and find them when they'd done their utmost to cover their tracks.

They had a bug aboard. But where? Was it amongst the computer and supplies they'd salvaged from the installation, or was the problem a deeper one? The humans were gone. So unless they'd carried a tracking device and planted it somewhere on the ship, that left only one possibility. Did they have a spy?

He'd not jested earlier about the attempts to use their computers to send a message. At the time he'd suspected one of the humans was trying to contact friends or family back on earth. However, with the humans all gone, that left only one disturbing prospect. A cyborg spy. The question was, did the spy know and willingly participate?

Please don't let it be Avion. He'd hate to kill his friend. He'd have to lay a trap and flush the traitor out.

"Lock down communications. All of them and jam our BCI to BCI frequency. We're going to verbal, face-to-face command only."

"But that will cut us off from the engine room."

"They know how to do their job, and I trust them to be able to handle themselves. Let's not give our possible traitor any more information than necessary."

"Aye, sir. What about the vessel following us? Do you want to try and lose it?"

"Like fuck." For one thing, they had Riley on board, and he wanted her back. And two… "They pissed off the wrong psychotic cyborg. Turn around, Aphelion. They want to fight, then by the rusted bolts holding my shit together, we'll give them one. Let's go kick some company ass."

Chapter Twenty Two

The explosions rocked the ship in a rather alarming fashion. It seemed the cyborgs weren't going to give in without a fight, or so Riley assumed. Ensconced in a cell, with no windows, no video screen, or anybody to ask what happened, she could only sit, listen, and hypothesize about the unfolding drama. From the percussions vibrating the floor, the muted thunder, and the occasional screams, it appeared violent.

Definitely more than Dennison reckoned on, she'd wager. Why he'd ever thought he'd prevail she didn't know. The cyborgs were heartless, killing machines. But not tough enough in the end.

Despite their reputation and the ease with which they'd infiltrated and taken over the installation, the cyborgs lost the battle. Hands cuffed behind their backs with thick metal restraints, heads bowed and faces bloodied, the mercenaries Dennison oversaw marched their prisoners into the holding area and locked them up. Riley recognized a few faces—Xylo and Avion among them —but also noted not all of the crew were accounted for. Probably because the fight wasn't completely over or so the vibration underfoot indicated, as something impacted the ship.

Please let Aramus be safe. Despite his treatment of her, she didn't wish him ill. If he suffered any harm, she wanted to inflict it!

In an ironic twist of fate, the fourth body dragged into the detention area was her ex-lover himself. Limp and bloodied, Aramus ended up thrown in the holding cell across from hers. He remained where they'd dumped him, an unconscious heap of flesh and metal that she desperately wanted to hate, yet couldn't.

She clung to the bars, face pressed against the cold metal, and willed him to move, to regain his senses, to give her a sign he lived. She'd even welcome an acerbic "Fuck off!" Then again, perhaps he was better off not regaining consciousness, not with what his future entailed. As a prisoner of the company, he was about to become an unwilling victim of experimentation for the second time in his life, this time with possibly deadly consequences. It seemed backward to hope that Dennison was right when he claimed their enhanced bodies could handle the abuse and merging with the alien DNA.

Because I don't think I can autopsy Aramus's body. But first he needed to live long enough to become a Frankenstein patient. He'd yet to move. Common sense tried to tell her they wouldn't put a corpse in a cell, but it wasn't until she saw him twitch several minutes after the soldiers left, joking about their victory over the not-so-tough cyborgs, that she breathed a sigh of relief, and when Aramus opened his eyes, she whispered a heartfelt, "Thank god."

"Don't you mean thank my nanos? Once again, they saved my metal ass."

"And here I thought it was your rock-hard head that saved the day," quipped Xylo.

Another joked, "Ha, it was his thick skin that kept him alive. Damn shit is so tough the bullets bounced off."

Tough? Having touched every inch of it, with more than just her fingertips, Riley begged to differ. Not that she'd tell him. Aramus didn't deserve any compliments, not when she was still mad at him for abandoning her.

Getting to his feet, Aramus rolled his wide shoulders and stretched, careful to not touch the bars, which hummed with electrical current. "Are you hurt?" he asked, as his eyes scanned her from head to toe.

"As if you care."

"More than I should," he muttered. "And you didn't answer my question. Are you injured? Have they hurt you?"

"Nothing other than a bump to my head when they wanted to shut me up. I'd ask if you're all right, but I'm sure that's a waste of breath, not to mention effort. Besides, I wouldn't want you to freak because I *care*." She said it with finger quotes before turning her back on him.

He chuckled, a low sexy rumble that made her senses vibrate in a way she tried to ignore. "I'm going to take a wild guess here and say you're angry."

Her? No. Which was why she didn't reply and stared at the wall. What an interesting wall. Rivets holding the seams. Scratches in the gray paint.

"Ignoring me won't make me go away."

Nope. But she enjoyed the childish satisfaction of it.

"Would it help if I said I was sorry and made a mistake?"

Yes! No, she wouldn't let him off the hook that easily. Actions spoke louder than words.

"I knew it as soon as we pulled away."

Yet he hadn't turned around. *He left me there. Alone. Unwanted.*

"I've missed you, even though it's only been ten hours and fourteen minutes since we last saw each other."

So what if he'd kept count? His computer probably kept a log of all events, even minor ones like dumping a human lover.

"Come on, Riley, talk to me."

She crossed her arms and really enjoyed her featureless view. It was only missing a few spots of rust to complete the ambiance.

"As soon as I heard about the attack, I turned around to come find you."

Ha. More like he wanted to make sure she and the others didn't spill any secrets.

"I know you're probably a little scared right now, and I just want you to know you don't need to worry. I'll get you out of here."

The snort escaped her before she could stifle it. Incarcerated too, exactly how did Aramus plan to rescue her?

He latched on to the sound. "I heard that. Are you doubting my ability to rescue you?"

She answered, despite her vow to remain silent. "Kind of hard not to, given where you are."

"You don't seriously think they can contain me?" Was that incredulity coloring his tone?

"They caught you didn't they, Mr. I'm-So-Bad-Ass?"

"Not exactly."

"Says the man in a cell."

"Only because I let them take me."

She whirled around, unable to resist. "Let them? Sure you did. Like I believe that. I know you, Aramus. I know it's not in you to let a human get the better of you. Or to care for you. God forbid a human do anything to the great and mighty cyborg Aramus."

"I am not that bad."

"No, you're worse." Because he'd made her fall for him and then done exactly what he'd promised—treated her like the enemy.

"You didn't used to think so."

"I changed my mind."

"Does this mean you won't want to copulate when I've freed you?"

"Is that all I am to you? A means for sex? You know what? I take back what I said. You're worse than a machine. Even a sex droid has more manners than you. I'll bet they have manners enough to say thank you too."

He approached the bars, close enough she feared him getting burned by the electricity coursing through them. "Thank you? Shouldn't you thank me? I worked my tongue and dick off making sure you got pleasure."

Of all the cocky things to say. "Yeah, you made me come, but so does my vibrator, and at least once it's done, it doesn't dump me on the floor or ditch me on a planet with barely a goodbye."

He winced. "I acted the fool."

"You were an asshole."

"Can we settle for jerk?"

"No."

"What will it take for you to forgive me?"

"Nothing, because I am not forgiving you, and we're never having sex again."

"I really wish you wouldn't lie like that."

She stomped her foot. "I don't lie."

"You just did because you will forgive me, and then we will have sex. Probably several times. In a row. And then the next day. Probably every day thereafter."

"Are not."

"Are too."

"Are not."

"Don't argue. If we're going to form a mating partnership, then we're going to need some ground rules. Rule number one, you must not make me seem weak in front of my brothers."

"Mating what?"

"Partnership. On earth, I believe religions cite it as marriage."

Jaw dropped and eyes wide, she stared at him. *He did not just say what I think he did.* "I am not marrying you."

"Of course not. I don't believe in god or religion. But we will register a civil bond with the cyborg department of interpersonal affairs so all know you belong to me."

"Oh my god. You are injured."

"Not according to my diagnostics."

"You must be because you are not making any sense."

"Oh, I am. Don't forget, I record everything, and in replaying our conversation, while you are doubting my word, which again, will have to stop if I am not to appear humanesculated in front of my brethren, I am making perfect sense. It has come to my belated attention, due to a loop that I only recently managed to break, that, although you are undoubtedly human, and fragile, I am still fond of you. I've tried to fight it. I've asked the doctor if I can be cured or operated on, but it seems there is no cure, lobotomy, or programming solution to my dilemma but one. I need to keep you."

"Or kill me."

His brows drew together. "No. That's not an acceptable course of action."

"But I'm human. Aren't we all supposed to die?"

"Only those responsible for the atrocities done to us. Oh, and anyone who lays a finger on you, cyborg or human. A male can handle only so much. I will, however, try to restrain myself from murdering those who look at you. Apparently, that crosses a line," he said with disgust.

It took her a moment to filter everything he said and read the underlying message he'd imparted in his usual backassed way. "Hold on a second. Is this your messed-up way of saying you love me?"

He nodded.

Her heart fluttered. "Say it."

"I'd rather not."

'Say it out loud, Aramus."

"But there are people coming, and my brothers are in the cells next to us," he hissed.

"An audience? Even better. Say it."

"You are testing my fucking patience, little doctor."

"Bite me."

"We've no time for foreplay. Later."

"Araaaamus." She drew out his name as she tapped her foot and crossed her arms.

"Very well. But I warn you, if anyone laughs, they will die. Probably painfully."

"Only if they deserve it."

He growled. "Stubborn human. It's a good thing I am fond of you."

"Still waiting."

"Fine. I love you. Are you content now? Can we move on?"

"What's that? I didn't quite understand you." She held her hand up to her ear and pretended she strained to hear.

"I. Love. You." The gritted teeth added a touch of eloquence to his words.

"Huh? My poor human ears. They just don't hear that well."

"I love you, Riley Carmichael!" He shouted just as Dennison and a cadre of soldiers turned the corner.

Only in her messed-up world would Riley finally get the declaration she wanted just as fate, with all its promised violence, came calling.

"Isn't that touching?" Dennison sneered. "A machine loving a fleshy. Will you still love her after I've fucked her in front of you?"

Aramus clenched his fists at his side, his face a mask of fury. "You are already slated to die. Threaten her again, or touch her in any way, and it will be painful. Your choice."

"Big threat for a cyborg behind bars."

"These? Bah. They won't hold me."

"If you're so big and mean, then how come we caught you so easily?"

"Who caught who?" A smile stretched Aramus's lips, and Riley took a step back, excited and chilled at the same time. The mocking grin Aramus wore, along with the gleam in his eyes, was the stuff cyborg legends were born of, psychotic with a dash of danger.

"Nice bluff. We know how to deal with your kind now. The previous cybernetic units we captured proved invaluable in our research. For example, those bars you mock, they're electrified. One touch and you'll fry the flesh off your bones faster than your nanos can heal, not to mention scramble your BCI. But feel free to try. Just try not to scream louder than your girlfriend over here. I'd hate to miss hearing them as I fuck her."

Talk about waving a red flag in front of a bull. Steam practically poured from Aramus's ears, but Dennison didn't pay him any mind as he advanced on her cell, a taunting leer on his lips. Riley retreated until her back touched the wall. Despite Aramus's boast, she didn't see a way out. Dennison held the upper hand. With soldiers at his back, he could do whatever he damn well pleased. Fighting would just make everything worse. She'd seen the results first-hand during her first incarceration. She'd just close her eyes and try to think of Aramus's declaration as she bore the pain and humiliation. It was the disgust in Aramus's eyes after she wasn't sure she could handle.

The lock to her cell clicked, and the door slid open on its metal track with only a small grating sound. The soldiers who'd accompanied Dennison lined themselves on either side of the opening, guns holstered at their side, Tasers held pointing outward, their smirks clear. They wouldn't stop the rape about to happen.

She swallowed the knot of fear forming in her throat as Dennison took one step in. Two.

"I warned you," Aramus growled. "Stupid motherfucker."

There was a certain sound metal made when bent in ways never meant by nature, when one force went up against another, straining and pulling.

Screeeeeeech!

How loud it seemed. How unexpected. This, along with a few shocked "Holy shit!", made for a noise she could only describe as wonderful. The smell of flesh as it sizzled? That she could have done without, yet it didn't seem to bother Aramus as he put his boast into action.

He stepped from his cell, cracked his knuckles and growled, "Who wants to die first?"

Chapter Twenty Three

Aramus never understood why his enemies never took his advice. He warned them not to fuck with him. Warned the little prick to leave his female alone. Stupid humans, they just never goddamned listened, and he was done giving them fair warning.

The fear in Riley's eyes spurred him into action. Aramus wasn't about to let the asshole entering her cell hurt one hair on her stubborn head. Only he was allowed to yank her hair or make her cry, preferably in pleasure.

Beside, human or not, what male didn't want an opportunity to prove he was the biggest and toughest warrior around? A reputation like his didn't come from letting others come to the rescue. What was a little scorched flesh when it came to keeping the legend of Aramus, baddest motherfucking cyborg, alive? That and he loved seeing the whites of the bastards' eyes as they realized their foolishness—and faced their mortality.

Before, he'd had to temper himself, let the human militia that boarded his ship think they held the upper hand. He'd not completely agreed with the plan when Aphelion first proposed it, but he had to admit it made the most sense. If he wanted to ensure they didn't massacre Riley or any other prisoners on board, then he needed to get on the enemy ship and find out where they'd stashed them. The best way to accomplish that was as a captive.

So the cyborgs engaged their pursing enemies in a mock battle. Not too fake. He didn't want to rouse their suspicions, especially not when he knew they harbored a spy, but not intense enough to cause permanent damage to either vessel or its passengers.

The fact he ended up in a detention cell across from Riley proved an unexpected bonus. It checked off a few items on his to-do list. Of course, the way she got him to admit he loved her in front of an audience, something he'd never live down, meant his list got longer as now he'd have to kill those who'd overheard.

Which can be arranged. He'd miss his brothers, Xylo especially, who'd snickered the entire time he'd conversed with Riley. But he'd get over it.

Or he could let his brethren live and swear them to silence. Threaten them with a visit from his iron fists or, even more horrifying, threaten to sic that crazy cyborg female Deidre on them. The female would not leave him alone. She seemed determined to bed him, despite his numerous refusals. But now wasn't the time to mull over his plan already in motion. With danger courting his female, he needed to act.

It was almost too easy. Despite the boast of the slimy human in charge, there was no cell, electrified or not, that could hold him, not when his little doctor needed him. It seemed the company had not updated all of its personnel on the fact that cyborgs could resist electricity, or some of them at least could, like Aramus. During his last update, Einstein had modified his core programming and put him on a specialized regime that saw him playing with electricity on a regular basis, the dosage increasing each time, until he could handle more than the average cyborg. They'd learned their lesson with the Tasers the military used on them during a previous encounter.

The voltage still hurt as it coursed through his body, but he was cyborg. He wouldn't let it stop him, not when Riley needed him. He swallowed past the pain. The bars bent before his brute force with a high-pitched squeal. Out he stepped of his temporary cage. He cracked his knuckles as he asked who wanted to die first. Intimidation was always so much fun.

As usual, no one volunteered. *Pussies*.

"Don't just fucking stand there," screamed the idiot in charge. "Taser him."

As if remembering the devices they held, the hired thugs discharged them all at once. Only two actually hit Aramus, their electrical force coursing through his system. Not entirely pleasant. He forced a smile to his lips. "That tickles. Got anything stronger?"

"How the hell are you resisting it? They assured me the voltage would render you impotent."

"One, never ever use the word 'impotent' with me in the same sentence. Two, never underestimate a cyborg. We adapt. We always adapt. It is, after all, what we were designed for." That was the wonderful thing about being cyborg. If something broke or didn't work or, in this case, proved a weakness, then all it took was a programming tweak, some new hardware, and say hello to the new and improved cybernetic unit. He didn't mention the fact that only some of his kind got the specialized upgrades. With limited resources, not everyone could resist like he could.

"Don't just stand there. Shoot him!" screamed the idiot with bulging eyes.

It took a moment before the stunned soldiers aimed their weapons and fired. Aramus jerked as the bullets ripped through his flesh, some lodging in muscle, while others went right through. Fucking ill-trained mercs. Didn't they know only a headshot, and a very precise one at that, could take out a cyborg?

The plink of a bullet hitting the floor as his body repelled them, echoed in the suddenly silent space. "Ouch. That stung," he rebuked, his flesh already closing over the holes, his nanos humming as they worked.

Now their eyes showed the panic and realization that perhaps they'd fucked up. The hired soldiers raised their guns to fire again. Too slow. Aramus bashed their heads together before they could take a second shot. Then he went to work or, as Seth liked to joke, had grown-up playtime with his new squeaky toys.

He could have stripped their weapons from their hands and used them and freed his brothers, who clapped and whistled, but that would mean sharing the fun. So he went it alone, punching soft flesh, feeling bone crunch, hearing the grunts and gasps of men who thought they were tough until they met someone nastier than them. They soon learned the error of their ways. Pity for them that they didn't live long enough to truly enjoy the lesson.

A scream from Riley drew his attention as the little prick who'd taunted him held her in a chokehold across his body, using her as a shield. *Oh no he fucking didn't.*

"Move and she dies," his target threatened.

"How did a dumb fucker like you ever get put in charge?" Aramus, with reflexes faster than any human, snagged a gun from a blubbering soldier and fired.

Riley screamed as the three-eyed corpse wrapped around her sagged to the floor, dragging her with it. Aramus darted forward and pulled her into the safety of his arms. She trembled in his grip but, at the same time, clung tight to him, safe and sound. "Told you I'd get us out of here." Yeah. He sounded smug. Nothing like being right and saving the day to remedy a man's injured arrogance—and to remind those who'd been witnesses to his earlier ignoble admission that he still had what it took to kick their asses.

She hiccupped a sob as she sagged in his arms. "I hate you. No. I love you. You are such an arrogant, idiotic, handsome asshole of a man."

He ignored most of her speech and focused on the only important part. "But you love me?"

"Yes."

"And you will register for a civil bond with me?" Making her his in the eyes of the law and clarifying her status would also give him a line of defense when he killed the cyborgs who attempted to flirt with her.

"Yes."

"We will have copious amounts of sex," he declared.

"Don't push it."

"Oh, I will, deeply and thoroughly." How easy the innuendos came when he didn't fight against his more human side.

"How can you think of sex when we haven't escaped yet."

"Minor detail. Be sure to stand behind me while I take over the ship."

"Are you insane? You're injured. Let's free the others to do it."

"And let them have all the fun?" He didn't quite pout, but it was close.

"I think you should do as she says," Xylo taunted. "Let someone else get the most kills for once. You can go cuddle with your human while we clean up the mess."

"Can we get rid of him and make it look like an accident?" she asked.

"Easily," Aramus replied with a dark chuckle.

"Hey. Not funny," Xylo complained.

She laughed, the sweetest sound ever. "Fine. I won't let him kill you, so long as you keep him safe."

"I don't need his help." Aramus glared.

She smiled in the face of his annoyance. "While I am sure you could take over this ship all by yourself, we have more important things to do, such as locate Deidre."

"Why?" He'd done his best to shake the annoying female.

"Because she is a spy."

"But she hates humans."

"She hates everyone. It's part of her programming. It's why you didn't suspect her. But logic says it has to be her because Avion is here with us."

"We rescued another male as well, who is currently unaccounted for. It could be him."

She shook her head. "Call it a gut instinct."

In other words, trust her. Looking down at her, he nodded. "MJ!" he yelled for his medic. "Get over here."

"Just as soon as you let me out. Not all of us have gotten the new upgrades yet," reminded the cyborg.

Aramus quickly released his brethren and the few other prisoners, Percy included, as sirens blared. He'd just finished unlatching the last cage when the thump of boots echoed from around the corner. He tucked Riley behind him, using his body as a shield, and just in time too, as the mercenaries showed up, weapons firing erratically.

"Take them out," he yelled. "Before they—" The hiss and suctioning wind hit before he could finish his sentence. "—cause a breach." Fuck. While the lack of oxygen wasn't a big deal to him because he could regulate his body to survive without air, Riley, on the other hand, couldn't.

"Someone take care of the stuttering moron while the rest of you subdue this ship. I need to get Riley to safety." Tossing her over his shoulder, he pushed his way through the tussling bodies in search of an environmental suit or passage back to their vessel, whichever he located first.

She gasped on his back, silent for once, cognizant of the danger and not letting her usual stubbornness stand in the way of what he had to do. She didn't say a word, even as he grabbed a soldier who stepped from a room dressed in full space gear, snapped his neck, and proceeded to strip him.

She did utter a soft, "Thank you," as he stuffed her into the helmet and suit.

Chaos held a free rein as the enemy craft added computerized warnings to the blaring sirens. "Hull breach. Sealing passages in section 4F through nine in order to contain it in thirty seconds. All personnel are to evacuate those areas. I repeat…"

Assuming his brothers were smart enough to get out on their own, he concerned himself with his most important task. Getting Riley off this ship. No longer worried about her ability to breathe, he nevertheless hoisted her once again—she weighed nothing to him after all—and traced a circuitous route to where his BCI told him the ships were joined together. Having feigned unconsciousness during his foray on board, he had to rely on his computer instead of memory, which would have worked well if he'd known the idiosyncrasies of the craft he was on.

A wall with a locked door, a new one according to schematics, blocked his way. "Fuck me. Stupid builders not updating their goddamned records." He didn't want to waste time backtracking. He aimed his pistol at the control panel and fired. The circuitry spat and sizzled, the smell of burnt wires permeating the air. It didn't open the door. However, the ragged hole revealed a glint of orange, the color used to identify emergency levers hidden behind the crackling mess. He reached in and yanked. With a grind of metal, the portal slid open, and he stepped into a storage room filled with about six capsules, stasis chambers meant for flesh. All of them blinked numbers and lights indicating they were active.

"Who do they have in those?" Riley asked, her voice muffled by the helmet.

"I don't know, but we'd better try and get them out of here before the company decides we're better off not finding out." He didn't want a repeat of the installation where all of his witnesses got terminated before he could question them or bring them home for study.

He sent out a wireless message to Aphelion. *Hey, I've found something.*

So handle it, snapped his first mate. *I'm kind of busy.*

Stop playing with the mercs and get some units to hustle their metal asses over here. I might have found some intact test subjects, but we'll need to move them from this ship to ours.

Ruin a cyborg's fun, why don't you? Aphelion grumbled. *Do you know how long it's been since I got to practice with real soldiers instead of simulations?*

You'll be practicing with one hand if you don't fucking obey. Or did you miss the newest announcement?

While they argued, the enemy craft's computer had started playing a new message. "Self-destruct sequence activated. Four minutes thirty seconds until core meltdown."

Damn. They'd have to move, and quick. He set Riley down and took a closer look at the capsules. He hoisted one. Heavy, too heavy for him to run with, protect Riley, and get back to the ship and return for more.

A tap on his shoulder had him growling, "I'm a little busy right now."

"Yeah, but while you're busy weightlifting, I thought I should mention these stasis chambers have wheels and these cool gizmos called motors to turn them."

He peeked down. So they did. "Smartass."

Her muffled laughter didn't ease his annoyance. "Always glad to help. You guide one, and I'll follow with another."

Kentry, who arrived in a stomp of boots with Xylo at his back, took two more. In the end, they managed to recover five of the sleep units before they had to pull away from the vessel about to self-destruct.

They also brought along a few extra passengers, some new faces, some familiar—and some unwelcome.

Aramus dealt with them first.

Chapter Twenty Four

Back on board and in one miraculous piece. Since her rescue, Aramus refused to let Riley leave his sight. Even after they boarded his ship and he barked out orders, preparing them to disengage and set a course to somewhere safe, he insisted she remain with him. She didn't argue. After everything she had gone through, it felt nice to be wanted. Of course, Aramus didn't phrase it that way. His excuse was, "The spy is still at large."

But if he wanted to use Deidre as his reason for seating her on his lap as he snapped commands, who was she to gainsay him?

A few of his shipmates raised a brow at his breach of cyborg protocol, but none dared speak, probably because he glared at anyone who even looked her way.

Once they'd cleared the airspace and zone of impact expected from the self-destructing enemy ship, Aramus wasted no time in calling forth their newly rescued passengers. Percy entered the command center along with Carmen. Just like a rat, the two faced female saved her skin.

Percy at least wasted no time showing his gratitude. "Th-thank you for saving me."

"Don't thank me. It wasn't my idea." On the contrary, it seemed this Joe person who oversaw most of the cyborg affairs, had asked them to bring back anyone who might prove useful to their home planet. "Since you seem to have not been involved in the subterfuge involving the company, you may go to your room. I warn you though," Aramus leaned forward and fixed Percy with a stern glare. "Keep yourself out of trouble or, orders or not, I will eject you from my ship."

Head bobbing and Adam's apple bobbing, Percy almost ran out of the command center, Carmen, quiet for once, stuck close to his heels, obviously hoping that command applied to her too. Think again.

"Not you, woman. Get your treacherous ass back here."

Carmen froze, and when she turned, the snake had tears welling in her eyes, and her lower lip trembled. "I didn't mean to betray anyone. They made me. Threatened me to help or else."

"Liar." Riley couldn't help but comment.

Aramus didn't fall for her fake explanation either. "Did you, or did you not, conspire with the company?"

"Yes, but I had no choice."

"Did they hold a gun to your head?"

"Not quite."

"Lock you in a cell and threaten you with rape?"

"No, but—"

"I don't need to hear excuses. You, with foresight and malice, contacted the company and had them attack the space station. You knowingly divulged information about the cyborgs. You put Riley in danger. None of that is acceptable. Xylo?"

"Yes, sir?"

"Take the lying female and toss her out the airlock."

"What?" Riley exclaimed at the same time as Carmen.

Riley turned her shocked gaze on her lover. "Aramus, what are you doing? You can't just kill her."

"Why not?" He meant that in all seriousness. "She led to your recapture. She collaborated with the company. She will probably betray us all at the first opportunity. What else can I do?"

What indeed? Riley didn't know the answer. On the one hand, killing the other woman seemed cruel. Yes, she'd proven herself a snake, working with the enemy, but to kill her like this? So coldly? So—

With a scream of rage, Carmen launched herself at Aramus, the pointy tip of the knife they'd once again forgotten to strip from her, leading the way. "Die, you fucking robot!" screamed the Latina.

Riley didn't even think twice. She lunged at Carmen, hands reaching for the knife. The slice across her flesh didn't immediately hurt, but the blood flowed fast and free.

Stunned, Riley sank to her knees, watching as her essence dripped while behind her Aramus bellowed, "No!"

She barely noted the brief scuffle as Carmen was subdued and carted off, screaming invectives. Darkness overtook her.

Chapter Twenty Five

When Riley's lids fluttered open, she found Aramus at her bedside, face over hers, his eyes boring a hole. "About time you woke up," he growled.

"Nice to see you too," she murmured. "What happened?" Last thing she recalled was her ignoble faint at the sight of her blood.

"You were a fucking idiot. What were you thinking throwing yourself in front of me like that?"

"I was protecting you." Okay, so it sounded dumb when she said it aloud, and the twin brows that shot up on his forehead attested to it.

The incredulity was probably called for too. "You were what? You do realize that nothing short of a sword decapitating me would have actually done me permanent harm?"

She winced. "Yeah, well, I wasn't thinking at the time, just reacting."

"You are human."

"I am well aware of that. Thanks for reminding me."

"Apparently you do need reminding. I am built to handle danger. You are not. Do not ever, *ever*, put yourself in danger like that again. Do you know what it did to me to see you injured and bleeding like that? It hurt, Riley. I hurt! Don't you understand how defective you've made me? Even the thought of losing you is enough to make me unfit. I need you. " His voice actually broke on the last bit.

Suddenly, she found herself blinking back tears. "I'm sorry. Or not. I can't say I won't do the same again. I love you, Aramus. Tough cyborg or not, I can't help but want to protect you."

"If you feel a need to coddle me, then do so with less dangerous things."

"Like?"

"Xylo's cooking when we run out of rations. Or from Seth when he does laundry and uses too much soap. It chafes."

She couldn't help but smile. "I guess asking you to stay away from danger is too much to ask."

A pained expression creased his face. "Anything but that."

"I won't promise, but I'll try. Next time, given the choice between me getting knifed and you, I'll step aside."

"Good. And that goes for bullets too."

"Are you planning to go to war?"

"I won't go searching for one, if that's what you're asking, but neither will I run. My people need me on the front lines, protecting them."

"I won't let you go alone."

"Good. I think it's better if you're where I can keep a watch over you."

"Why? Don't you trust me?"

His brows drew together. "You misunderstand. I don't trust my brethren, and Joe would probably get mad if I killed off most of our colony for lusting after you, especially since it wouldn't be their fault."

A backward way of saying he found her attractive, but she'd take it. She'd take anything this big, brash cyborg gave her because she loved him. "How long until the doctor releases me?" she asked, peeking at her bandaged arm, which didn't hurt.

"Now. He says the wound was shallow and stitched it up tight. He's numbed the area and applied a topical unguent that will speed the healing process."

"So why are we still here?" She raised a brow. "Didn't someone promise me tons of copulation once he rescued me?"

"I am a cyborg of my word." Sweeping her into his arms, Aramus strode to the door, which slid open before him.

Riley had to ask. "What happened to Carmen?"

"She's dead. By her own hand."

She gasped. "What?"

"When her attack on me didn't succeed, the crazy female turned the knife on herself, slashing the arteries in both thighs. She died before we could stop the bleeding."

"Oh, my god. I can't believe she committed suicide."

Aramus shrugged. "I'm not. She knew she was slated for death. She just chose the method and did it on her terms."

It didn't make it any less gruesome. "And what about Deidre?"

"That was ugly. It took four of my crew to subdue her. But you were right. She was a spy."

"So she confessed?"

"Not exactly. However, Aphelion found the makings of a bomb in her chamber as well as attempts to contact unidentified vessels. Thankfully, none went through because of the blocks I had put into place. We've got her in holding currently, where she is screaming the end of days is coming for both humans and cyborgs. She is also causing herself damage."

"What are you going to do to her?"

Sadness, an emotion she was sure Aramus was unaware of, creased his craggy features. "I don't know. Her programming is corrupt. Her emotions out of control. She injured cyborgs during her capture and has vowed to kill us all because we are unnatural. We might have to terminate."

"But she's cyborg. Can't you just wipe her clean, and I don't know, reboot her?"

"Too many things have been done to her. Too much damage. I don't know if we have the parts necessary to repair. The decision will be left to the colony. In the meantime, she will be placed in stasis."

"Using those capsules we found?"

He nodded.

"But don't they already have passengers?"

"Not for long. MJ is waking one of them as we speak. A cyborg unit, or so the manifest claims."

"You don't want to be there when this person awakes?"

"Time enough to meet them later. As a certain human reminded me, I made a promise. And I am a cyborg of my word." Aramus grinned, probably because they'd reached his quarters and, more importantly, his bed.

He placed her upon it and began divesting her of her dirtied jumpsuit.

So much had happened though, and much of it had layered her skin in grime she couldn't stand. "Can we shower first?"

"Can't we shower after?" he grumbled.

"I'll make it worth your while," she teased, rising from his bed and tossing a sultry look over her shoulder as she strolled to his bathroom.

As commander of the vessel, Aramus's quarters boasted a larger shower unit than the other rooms. Big enough for two.

She stood under the warm spray, careful to keep her bandaged arm out of the water because waterproof or not, she didn't want to have to go back to the sick bay. Head tilted back, face taking the brunt of the warm spray, she felt him step in behind her, his big body dwarfing hers. His hands spanned her waist and the tip of his erection poked at her lower back. She couldn't help a little wiggle.

"Riley." He groaned her name.

"Where's that famous cyborg control?" she teased.

"Non-existent where you are concerned."

She turned in his arms and smiled at him. "You say the nicest things."

"Only you would claim that when I admit to being defective."

Laughter spilled from her. "Desire is not a defect. Only coming before I'm done is."

His lips quirked. "Is that a challenge?"

"Let's see how much you can take before you beg me to stop."

"I don't beg."

"We'll see." Down to her knees she dropped, the angle of the spray hitting Aramus's chest and rolling down his defined abs. But it wasn't his rock-hard stomach she wanted. It was his cock. It bobbed before her, eager for attention, and she was more than ready to give it some.

First, though, some of the teasing she promised. She gripped it at the base, enjoying the silken texture over a rod of steel. Stroking it up and down, she marveled, not for the first time, at the size. He truly had a cock to make any man envious.

Leaning forward, Riley flicked her tongue against the swollen head. That earned her a groan, so she lapped at it again, bathing his shaft with her tongue, licking it up and down, treating it like the most savory of treats. Oh, the guttural sounds he made at her actions. She swirled her tongue around the fat head of his dick before she took him in her mouth, his width a tight fit.

"Oh, fuck me." He moaned the words as his fingers threaded through the wet strands of her hair, his hips thrusting in time to the back-and-forward motion of her sucking.

She worked his cock with her mouth, her cheeks hollowed as she suctioned him. Mmm, did he ever enjoy that judging by his raspy breathing. While one of her hands gripped the base of his shaft, she used the other to play with his balls, rolling them between her fingers. His hips arched, and he somehow got even thicker.

The more excited he got, the more her own desire grew. She knew if she touched herself she'd find her pussy wet and ready for him. But she'd vowed to make him beg. So, she continued to suck and play and lick until…

"You win," he said in a hoarse voice. "I can't take it anymore. I need to fuck you."

Thank god, because she wanted the same thing—now!

She rose and pivoted at the same time, placing her hands on the wet shower wall and angling forward enough to present her bottom. His hands grasped her hips as his feet nudged her feet farther apart. He rubbed her clit with his engorged tip and she moaned.

She gasped. "Now who's being a tease?"

He slammed his shaft home, and she let out a cry of pleasure.

Damn, that feels good.

His long, thick cock filled her, the throbbing width buried balls deep inside of her, stretching her. Oh, how she liked it when he swirled his hips, grinding his cock head against her G-spot. Back and forth, he seesawed, each penetration finishing with an extra wiggle that made her convulse before he withdrew. Then he started over again.

His body curved over hers as he thrust, and one of his hands reached under to find her clit, pinching it. Sensation overload! She cried out as her body jerked, the force of her orgasm gripping her by surprise and shaking her. Shuddering waves wrapped around his cock, each squeeze making her whimper then cry out again as he pulsed within her, his climax triggered by hers.

Chest heaving, bodies joined, he said it, without prompting, without threat.

"I love you. For as long as my heart beats. Which, given the battery life on the sucker is a few hundred years, will be a very long, fucking time."

"I love you too, Aramus." And she did. Aramus might think he was more machine than man, but she knew better. Mechanical heart or not, cyborgs felt, and cyborgs could love, even a human like herself.

Epilogue

Basking in the afterglow of sex, make that lovemaking because adding emotions to the act made it transcend anything as basic as sex, Aramus wanted to ignore the repeated buzzes of people trying to get his attention. For once, he intended to ignore duty and act selfishly. Unless the ship was on fire or they were under direct attack, the distractions could wait. He was doing well too at his first bout of selfishness and had almost fallen asleep, with Riley atop him, when the door to his room slid open.

What the fuck? No one should have been able to override his lockdown request. No one but—

"Seth!" He growled the name, happy, and yet not, to see the irritating cyborg step into his room. "Where the fuck did you crawl out of?"

"I was a passenger on the ship you just acquired. I take it you didn't read the captain's log. I was enjoying a lovely, restorative nap in one of their stasis capsules, not entirely by choice, when MJ woke me. He told me you were busy getting your rocks off with a human. I assumed he was delirious, but when repeated slaps to his head to jolt his synapses didn't change his story, I had to come see for myself."

The lost cyborg hadn't changed at all. Just as irritating as ever. "Go away."

"But you haven't even introduced us yet." Seth waggled his brows at Riley, who bit her lip, probably so she wouldn't giggle. It wasn't hard to see the mirth in her eyes.

However, Aramus wasn't in the mood to share her yet, especially given the only thing she wore was a thin sheet. "Who she is, is none of your business."

"Aw, come on, Aramus. Don't be like that. Aren't you just the teensiest, tiniest bit glad to see me?"

Yes, but he'd never admit it. "Not really. It was a lot more quiet and peaceful with you gone."

"Funny. I would have said the same thing myself." The new voice took them all by surprise. A strange woman crowded into Aramus's room, a statuesque blonde whose gaze alit with interest on Riley. "If it isn't the forensic doctor. I've got questions for you."

"And I have a question too. Just who the fuck are you, lady, and what do you want?"

Seth beamed, looking entirely too pleased with himself. "I think introductions are in order. Aramus, and hot-looking naked girl in his bed, I'd like you to meet Anastasia. My wife."

"Ex."

"Now, darling, you know I don't believe in divorce."

"And I'm fine with becoming a widow." With those words, Anastasia, in a blur of movement, took Seth to the floor and held a gun to his head. Holy shit. Aramus never thought he'd see the day when someone could best their wiliest fighter.

Only an insane cyborg like Seth would grin and say, "Isn't she wonderful?"

What was wonderful was Riley's laughter. *My woman.* The one human capable of teaching him that love wasn't always a weakness. And, if anyone dared to say otherwise, he had an iron fist to help adjust their thinking. He did have a reputation to maintain after all.

The End...
...but the saga continues with SETH.

Made in the USA
Columbia, SC
17 June 2017